Booty in the Backseat

by

Karen C. Whalen

*The Tow Truck Murder Mysteries,
Book Six*

Copyright Notice
This is a work of fiction. Names, characters, places, and incidents are either the product of the author's imagination or are used fictitiously, and any resemblance to actual persons living or dead, business establishments, events, or locales, is entirely coincidental.

Booty in the Backseat

COPYRIGHT © 2024 by Karen C. Whalen

All rights reserved. No part of this book may be used or reproduced in any manner whatsoever without written permission of the author or The Wild Rose Press, Inc. except in the case of brief quotations embodied in critical articles or reviews.
Contact Information: info@thewildrosepress.com

Cover Art by *Diana Carlile*

The Wild Rose Press, Inc.
PO Box 708
Adams Basin, NY 14410-0708
Visit us at www.thewildrosepress.com

Publishing History
First Edition, 2024
Trade Paperback ISBN 978-1-5092-5798-0
Digital ISBN 978-1-5092-5799-7

The Tow Truck Murder Mysteries, Book Six
Published in the United States of America

Dedication

To my husband Tim who came up with the title.

Acknowledgements

A huge thank you to beta reader Sandra Hilger, plus my fellow Wild Rose authors Rhonda Blackhurst and Pamela Kyel, and the members of the Coastal Writers Group. I also appreciate my editor at The Wild Rose Press, Ally Robertson, and cover artist, Diana Carlile. Also, a special thanks to my readers.

Chapter 1

It's not a good idea to park in a no-parking zone. It's a worse idea when the no-parking zone is in the alley behind Main Street, because when you leave your car there, I get the call.

I entered the alley fast. Mike Horn waved to me from his loading dock, then gestured over to the black Volvo parked illegally in the tow-away zone. My high-heeled shoe pumped the brake as I cranked the wheel and slid my red tow truck behind the vehicle. The Fulcan Xtruder came perfectly in line with the tow as you would expect of a top-of-the-line unit.

Mike put a hand to his mouth and shouted, "Can you move the Volvo? I'm expecting a delivery any moment now."

I gave him a thumbs up and he disappeared through the door of the old red-brick building. The Volvo was reversed-in to the graffiti-covered concrete dock. I paged through my vehicle encyclopedia for the T8 model, a classy-looking cross between a sedan and a SUV.

Mike leaned out the door, tapped on his watch, and shook his head before returning inside. I flipped back and forth in my book a few more times, becoming frantic now. Encountering an expensive electric car like this was unusual, but I should know this stuff without having to look it up.

It was June, the height of tourism season, and all the

businesses on Main Street were hopping busy. The alley was a convenient place to snug away a car and avoid a parking meter. I swung my gaze over my shoulder, hoping the car's owner didn't show up to hassle me. I wasn't up for the usual insults that accompanied pissed-off drivers.

Finally locating the car in my encyclopedia, I bent the spine back to study the fine print. Since the drive shaft could be either front or rear wheel, I needed to lift both ends. My self-loading tow truck raised only one end with the nifty wheel-lift system that operated hydraulically from inside the cab. So, I pressed the button on the controller that lowered the T-shaped crossbar and extended the curved claws around the front tires. I got out of the truck and fixed my tow dollies onto the Volvo's rear tires and pumped those up. My tow dollies lifted the back, the boom elevated the front, all wheels were off the ground, and I was ready to roll.

Ohhhh yeah. Not bad, not bad at all.

I'll admit I had been struggling to learn the business for a while now. There's more to it than you might think. For instance, I had to learn which vehicles were front-wheel drive and which were rear wheel. If only I didn't feel like an imposter, lil' ole me driving this big ole truck, competing with the good-ole-boys in town. I'm a twenty-eight-year old woman in a man's world. At least I'm unique, since I'm the only female tow truck driver in Spruce Ridge, and better yet, I'm known as the high-heeled driver. I fell into the towing business when I inherited the truck from my absent dad, then I'd earned a reputation when I'd forgotten to change out of heels before arriving at my first tow. Now when I get a call, people ask for the high-heeled driver and that's okay with me. I liked being one of a kind, even if the image is not anything I'd planned. Isn't that how things happened? An accidental journey into an unanticipated life.

Might as well embrace it. I had a black stiletto painted on the truck door as my brand. That's me. That's who I am now. Delaney Morran, present owner and operator of Del's Towing.

After I deposited the Volvo behind the secure gate at Oberly Motors, I tapped the button on the remote and the car's front tires lowered to the ground with a soft *pumpf*. I got out to deflate the tow dollies and lock them back in the storage brackets, then pressed another button to retract the claw-like components and fold the boom onto the truck bed. Once that was done, I pulled out my phone to take a photo of the VIN for my records.

The tinted windows caused me to turn on the camera's flash. The inside of the vehicle lit up when I snapped the picture of the unique jumble of letters and numbers that identified the vehicle, and something in the backseat caught my eye. An odd shape. What was it? Alarm bells went off in my mind. I needed to make sure I hadn't transported a napping person or a sleeping dog or who-knows-what else. You see all kinds of things in the car hauling business.

I walked around to the rear passenger side and cupped my hands against the glass. Two dark blue duffle bags rested on the seat, one partly unzipped. There was cash inside. Lots of cash. Overflowing with cash. Bundles of fifties wrapped in brown bands and one hundreds in dark yellow ribbons.

Hunh. Imagine that.

I tested the door. It was unlocked.

What to do?

So…I'm basically an honest person. Sure, there was the one time I stole a glittery hairband from the most popular girl in middle school, but that was because she made fun of my red braids and called me that flame-haired girl. Don't disrespect a girl's hair. So she got what was coming to her. Besides, I returned her hairband the next day. This money was on a different level. Like felony level. I could go to jail instead of the principal's office.

There was no way I would lift any of the cash, but an unjustified guilt swept over me anyway. What if the vehicle owner accused me of making off with a couple hundred? Would I need to prove I didn't?

No matter what, I couldn't leave the car here with this kind of money inside, even if my impound lot was secure behind the razor-wired fence. The vehicle and contents were now my responsibility. I hadn't encountered anything like this before and could use some advice.

Should I call Ephraim Lopez? The county sheriff from whom I was taking a break, that cheating so-and-so. But as far as I knew, no law had been broken here, and Ephraim would think I'm trying to get back together with him.

Should I call Tanner Utley? The hot tow truck driver who taught me the business. Tempting, tempting, but I couldn't call on an old beau for help as soon as I'd broken up with the last one.

Should I call Zachariah Bowers? A Spruce Ridge police officer well known to me. The only thing is, I could picture his lecture all too well. He'd blame me for butting my nose into another suspicious situation. But, since he's with law enforcement he'd know what to do, and since I didn't have his number, I called Kristen, his girlfriend and my closest friend.

My car lot's not far from the police station, and Zach showed up within minutes in his black and white. He flung his door shut and strode over. "Delaney, what's this about a car full of money?" His prominent chin, handlebar mustache, and premature salt and pepper hair distinguished him from every other city cop in a tan uniform.

"Over here." I led him through the secure gate to the black Volvo T8. Side by side, we stooped to peer through the dark window. "It's not locked," I pointed out.

"Get back." He tugged open the door, pulled the first bag to the edge of the seat, and gave out a long whistle. "I need to wait till the second officer gets here."

"You called for backup?"

"Standard procedure, so no one can claim I helped myself to a few bills."

"No one would think that." Of course I'd worried about the same thing, but I'd never believe it of Zach.

Zach was a churchgoing, aboveboard, decent man, and that's why he was with my friend, Kristen, who lived her faith, helped those in need, never told a lie, and all that. In other words, she was ten times a better person than me. Zach and Kris were good people and made a great couple.

A squawk came from the mic on his shirt collar. While he talked to the dispatcher, I crept forward for a closer look. I poked the duffel with my finger. When he got off the mic, I asked, "What's that?"

He donned latex gloves. "Money."

Duh. "I mean underneath?" I squinted into the open

bag, my nose breathing in the dirty scent of used bills and something else equally nasty.

He jiggled the bag and the stacks of cash bounced around revealing something farther down. We both inched closer, in slow motion, as if afraid a spider among the bills was going to jump out and bite one of us.

Zach cried out, "Good grief, it's a severed hand."

"A hand? Severed? From a body?" I felt the blood drain from my face and nearly fell off my heels.

"Yes, a right hand. Step away from the vehicle, Delaney," Zach warned me. "Don't touch the door."

I practically screamed, "My prints are already all over it." I took a deep breath and let it out with a whoosh, glad Zach was here to handle this creepy development. He got back on the mic to request crime scene investigators for here and a team of investigators for the alley where the Volvo had been parked, once I explained I towed it from there.

When he got off, I said, "I'm going inside if you need me," then quick-stepped over to the auto body shop opposite my impound lot.

The motoring sound of an air compressor blasted from the auto bay along with a strong odor of paint fumes. Inside, dirty rags hung over the back of a folding chair, but I pulled the chair out anyway and plopped onto the creaky seat.

Byron Oberly was laboring over a Chevy Express van, rear-wheel drive. He lay down his paint gun to ask me, "What's goin' on?"

"Good morning to you, too, Old Man." That's what I called Byron. He'd never been married, as far as I knew, and didn't have any kids of his own. His nieces and nephews called him, "Old Man," so I did, too. "You won't believe this," I said.

"Don't tell me you found a dead body." Byron smiled with his gap-toothed grin. He was pushing fifty or even sixty, and heavyset, always in coveralls with a rag in the pocket. He rolled his eyes like it was a big joke.

"Well, um…" I twirled the end of my braid with my fingers, thinking how to say this. "There's like…like a chopped-off hand in a bag of money in the back of that car I towed. The Volvo I just brought in. I spotted the cash, but Zach found the hand, not me." If my words sounded defensive, they were.

He jerked his head. "What in the world?"

"I know." I popped my eyes wide.

"A chopped-off hand, like from a corpse?"

"I guess so."

"Come inside the office."

I rose from the folding chair and followed him through the door to a clean reception area with a comfy-looking, beige sofa. Car magazines covered a low, black table. A coffee machine with single-serve pods sat on a corner shelf. Crisp, green plants hung in baskets in front of the window. The mocha color on the walls was calming, more like a living room than the lobby of an auto body shop.

We stood at the window to watch the activity. Two more Spruce Ridge black and whites showed up and officers got out to join Zach. Before long, yellow tape surrounded the Volvo and a team of investigators wearing gloves were busy collecting evidence.

"So, tell me about it, Delaney. Start at the beginnin'. You better sit down." The hefty mechanic gestured toward the sofa. This shop had belonged to my dad before he died. I had inherited the truck. Byron Oberly had purchased the shop. I used the fenced part of the back of his lot as my impound space, so I'd gotten to know Byron fairly well. He often acted in the role of my father better than my actual father ever did. He was forever concerned about me.

I collapsed onto the couch. "I towed a car over here from behind Main Street. Mike called me to move it since he was expecting a delivery and it was blocking his loading zone."

"Mike Horn?" Byron lowered himself onto a stool behind the service counter.

"That's right. So, after I hauled it here…" I jerked a thumb at the window. "I went to capture the VIN on my phone and saw these bags in the backseat. One of the bags was open and there was money in it. Tied up in bundles. So I called Zach."

"You done right." His head bobbed.

"There was a severed hand inside with the money." I raised my shoulders and let them drop. "That's it. That's all I know about it."

Byron fished a rag out of the pocket of his overalls and wiped it across his forehead. "How you fall inta' this stuff is beyond me."

"Me too, Old Man, me too." My cheeks heated. Darn my tendency to blush.

We both turned as someone came through the front door.

"What up?" A teen in dirty, oversized sneakers, baggy jeans, and a knit cap let the door bang shut behind him. Axle Guttenberg, my friend Kristen's younger cousin, had Kristen's same gray eyes and thick, dark hair. He was an annoying teenager, but also a genius with anything mechanical, and Byron hired him away from another auto shop in town. Earbuds plugging his ears, Axle kept walking toward the auto bay as if this was just an average Tuesday.

"Axle, didn't you notice the police outside?" I asked him.

He stopped and yanked out an earbud. "Oh yeah, the cops swarming all over that killer Volvo."

I winced. "Killer? What do you know?"

"It's turbocharged, man. Why?" He narrowed his eyes.

"Take a seat and I'll tell you."

He slouched on the sofa next to me and flicked his gaze to Byron, who gave him a *don't-ask-me* look, then swiveled in my direction. He said, "Okay, spill," so I brought Axle up to speed on the hand we'd found. And the money. All the while Axle stared at me, open mouthed.

Byron said when I was done, "You know that car was involved in a crime, right Delaney? You're goin' ta stay well away from it, I hope."

"I'm in here with you, aren't I?'

"Too bad you called the cops. That cash could've come in handy. Get it? *Handy*." Axle laughed and gave me an elbow to the gut.

I groaned and swatted him back. "*Eeew*."

"Too soon?"

"Yes. And the cash is off limits. Probably stolen or something, like Byron said," I reminded Axle.

His eyes lit up. "Exactly right. So whoever stole that money is not going to call the cops to ask for it back."

"*Hellooo*. See the cops outside? Too late, so pass on that, lil' cuz'." I didn't admit that pocketing some of the cash had crossed my mind for a second or two.

The sounds of car doors slamming brought us to our feet and the three of us hurried over to the window. We watched all the officers depart except for forensics and Zach, who aimed in our direction. He entered the open auto bay and came through to the reception area.

"Hello, Byron, Axle." He nodded at them, then at me. "Delaney, I'm taking off, but forensics isn't done yet. When they leave, the crime scene tape stays up. No opening the vehicle. No meddling. No interfering. Right?"

"Right," I appeased him. In the absence of a city impound lot in this small town, I would be responsible to keep the Volvo secure in my lot until the police released it. After that, I could collect towing and storage fees from the vehicle owner when they came to pick up the car. I waited for more information, but Zach only nodded his big chin at me again, patted his duty belt, and turned to leave.

"Wait!" I shot out the door after him. "So, what did you find? The rest of the body wasn't in the trunk or something, was it?" I made a cringy face.

He stopped and planted his hands on his hips. "No more body parts in the vehicle."

"What about the alley where the car was parked? Did you hear if anything was found there?"

"The site is being searched as we speak, but, Delaney, the police will investigate this. You need to stay out of it." His mic screeched, making me flinch. "Gotta go." He keyed the mic and started talking while climbing into his patrol car.

I shook my head at Axle and Byron standing in the doorway, then shrugged a *who-knows-palm-up* gesture. The two men, one old and one young, gave each other side glances as if to say, *what did you expect,* before trudging back to the auto bay.

****

The next morning, Axle came down the hall, heading for the kitchen and the coffee maker. Since he was Kristen's cousin, that practically made him my cousin, too, and he rented my spare room, which helped me with the rent. What I helped him with was relationships, which mostly amounted to telling him to ditch the beanie and use deodorant. He was wearing a knit cap on his head as usual, but the silver chain around his neck was new.

"What's with the necklace?" I leaned against the cabinet, a steaming coffee mug to my lips.

His hand went to his neck. "What?"

"I like it. Did Shannon give you that?" I doubted Axle had enough good taste to pick out jewelry on his own. His girlfriend likely had an influence.

He lifted the silver cord to chin level and let it fall. "Yeah. That's dope, huh?"

"Uh-huh. Take your dog for a walk." I poured him a cup of joe, then rinsed the pot.

After Axle walked his Rottweiler, Boss, the two of us headed out for the day. Axle said, taking the stairs in front of me, "What's the word on the bags of cash?" He and I hadn't had a chance to talk more about it the night before.

"The only thing I know, there wasn't a cut-up body in the trunk to go along with that severed hand."

"Was it a right hand or left?"

"Right."

"Well, if you'd found a left hand, it just wouldn't be right."

It took me a moment, then I smacked him in the shoulder. "No shit? I mean, really?" I offered him my fiercest glare. "Dude, that is so cold."

"Fine," he smirked. "I see how you are." He'd reached the bottom of the stairway that led to the parking lot.

"What do you mean?" I skipped down the last few steps.

"You're too serious. Come on, Delaney, where's your sense of humor?" He poked me hard in the back and we regressed into pushing and shoving.

"I'm really not up for your crapola this morning." I looked longingly at the back door to Roasters on the Ridge Coffee Shop, instead of my Fiat parked beside it.

Roasters sat on the corner of Pine Street and Eagle Ave. No drive-through service, but a charming, trendy, and crowded coffee bar that roasted its own beans. And the best part was that we lived right above the shop. That's because Kristen owned Roasters and leased the entire building that included the two apartments on the second floor. Axle and I lived in the apartment across the landing from Kristen.

Axle took hold of my shoulders and directed me inside. "Go ahead. You know you want one."

Never one to turn down caffeine, I followed Axle through the employee entrance and across the tiny kitchen out to the front. Quaint signs greeted us, "Coffee makes everything possible," and "Humanity runs on coffee." Wall-mounted antique skis and poles, snowshoes, and ski boots provided a themed ambiance. Distressed wooden shelves held beans, mugs, and syrups. Most shops didn't want the expense and wasted space of a coffee roaster, but Kristen was a purist who roasted her own beans, and right now the roaster filled the café with cracking sounds and a heavenly fragrance of coffee.

"Morning, you two." Kris smiled from behind the cash register. She wore the café's black apron embroidered with a swirl of steam over a coffee mug. She had widely spaced gray eyes, dark shapely brows, and shoulder-length brown hair. How I envied her smooth, shiny hair. Who wouldn't? Especially someone like me with curly red hair—all right, orang*ish* hair, darn it—that I wore in a thick braid down my back. Not that I compared myself to Kris or anything.

"The usual?" she asked. I nodded as she started on my double shot espresso, then Axle's caramel latte.

Axle said to Kris, "Hey, you heard about yesterday?"

"Zach told me a little bit." She glanced at me with concern. "You okay?"

Axle grunted a laugh and reached across me for his latte. "This time instead of a body…" he said, pausing for dramatic effect, "Delaney found booty in the backseat."

Chapter 2

I choked on my hot drink, trying not to spit it all over myself, and waved my hand in Axle's face, like *stop talking already.*

"Nice one, Axle." Kristen's eyes rolled up toward the coffee shop ceiling.

I said, "Yeah. Who uses that expression? Booty?"

"Old people, like you." The teen popped in an earbud and fiddled with his phone. His music blared so loudly everyone could hear it. He was a typical eighteen-year-old male, and since Kris and I were ten years older, we felt ancient.

Kris said to me, "Zach called a few minutes ago. He's on his way over here if you want to talk to him."

"Maybe we'll stick around." I raised my eyebrows at Axle. "You have time?" He was depending on me for a ride because his used Altima, front-wheel drive, was on the fritz again. He was always taking it apart and rebuilding it. He didn't appear to be in a hurry, his head down, bopping to the music. "Looks like we can wait," I told Kris.

I shepherded Axle to the side, then unlocked my phone to start scrolling. A few minutes later, the door to the coffee shop opened and Zach stepped in.

I greeted him, "Hello, Officer Bowers," but he only had eyes for Kristen. After Kris and Zach exchanged smiles, he turned my way. "Might as well get this over with. Sheriff Lopez has taken over the investigation so don't try to ask me any questions."

He was on to me!

"I'll have your latte ready in a moment, Zach," Kristen told her boyfriend.

"Let's move out of the way." He led me to a table and Axle trailed behind.

I asked him, "Why did Ephraim take the case?"

"It could fall under 'major crime.' Body parts could mean a homicide." In Spruce Ridge, homicides were investigated by the county sheriff's department rather than the city police department, and the county sheriff assigned to this case was well known to me, Ephraim Lopez. My boyfriend from whom I was taking a break. Yup, him, the two-timer.

I said, "Maybe it's not murder. People can survive the loss of a hand."

"Without medical help, a person would bleed out, and no one was brought to the hospital with those kinds of injuries. We checked a wide area, including Denver. It's not like a Rambo movie. It's not like the victim could cauterize his own wounds."

"Especially with only one hand," Axle said, grinning.

I squashed a groan. "Any idea how this happened, Zach? Could it be drug or gang related?" There were drugs in this small town, just like everywhere else. And where there were drugs, there were gangs. I'd actually run across gang members before. I'd seen them right here in the coffee shop. Yes, right here in Spruce Ridge.

This mountain town, the gateway between Denver and Vail, has three distinct sections. The ginormous mansions on the mountain side where the celebrities and millionaires lived, the historical district near Main Street where the working class lived, and a newer area with subdivisions, strip malls, and big box stores. That's where the coffee shop is and where we live. The uber rich in their stately homes had plenty of money for recreational drug use. The dealers were usually from out of town, but the buyers were from here.

"Gangs?" Kristen walked up to the table with Zach's nonfat latte, horror registering on her face.

Zach accepted the lidded to-go cup. "Delaney, let it go."

"Let it go? Really? Really, Zach?"

Zach shook his head at me. "I already gave you more information than you need to know. Stay out of it, would you? Why do you have to keep your nose in?"

"Peace of mind, to keep informed, morbid curiosity, all of the above." I wasn't interested in a cop lecture, so I cut my eyes to Axle and said, "It's go time. You coming?"

Zach said, "Before you leave, there is something."

I spun around. "What?"

"The Volvo T8 has been released and the owner contacted. You'll probably get a call any time now. Owners are Rick and Courtney Rearden."

"*Suh-weet*. That was fast." I'd be glad to see the last of that Volvo. And get paid for the tow.

"Forensic stayed with it all night and finished up this morning. The money was taken as evidence."

"Did you talk to the owners?" I knew someone with that same last name, maybe a relative.

"Not me. Ephraim."

"Okay, thanks." I said my goodbyes, and Axle and I ducked out the door.

I hurried to keep up with Axle, then climbed behind the wheel of my Fiat, my little Italian job that looked something like a Smart Car. He slid into the passenger seat and buckled up. We breezed along Pine Street, right turned on Fifth, and rolled to a stop at Oberly Motors. Once Axle unwound himself from my car and entered the auto body shop, I pulled through the gate and parked next to my tow truck. The reason I stored the truck here was because Kristen would not want me to leave the big truck in the coffee shop parking lot overnight.

I unlocked the truck door and got in, immediately cocooned in the warmth of the self-loader.

My dad, Del Morran, had died in a hit-and-run accident, and the other driver had never been identified. But more mysterious than his accident was the fact Dad had left me his amazing self-loading tow truck. I didn't know my father when I was growing up. My parents divorced when I was seven, and I never saw him again. The man who fathered me left me his name, his Irish red hair, and his tow truck, but no memories. Although, the recognizable smell of motor oil and the woodsy scent clinging to the upholstery stirred a vague recollection. When I breathed in the truck aroma, I felt his presence, like he was sitting here with me. A comforting thought, affirming that I wasn't alone.

Not that I was totally on my own. Mom's image popped into my head. Her blonde hair styled in its usual short bob. Her perfect coif and pearls. Her predictable questions about my life and her comments about everyone else's. I hit her number on speed dial.

"Hello, Mom. How are you?" I asked when she picked up.

"Laney, I was just about to phone you."

"What for?"

"I'm going to be in Spruce Ridge tomorrow. You have time to meet your mother?"

I nodded at the phone. "Sure. Are you planning to go shopping?" Mom often spent time at the upscale stores in this affluent town, not too far from her home in Denver.

"No. I just want to visit with my daughter." She sounded odd.

"Everything okay?"

"Of course. How about with you?"

"Yeah, me too." I couldn't explain the whole money-*dash*-severed hand thing. I didn't have it in me right now, although it was soothing to hear her voice. "How's Will?"

"He's fine. See you tomorrow." Saying goodbye was usually a long process with Mom, but she'd hung up, so I deposited the phone back inside my purse.

I fired up the tow truck and the engine rumbled, making my heart glad as it always did, but I couldn't help but worry. Mom had not complained about the neighbors, shared gossip about my step-dad's law partners, or reminded me that I was underemployed and not using my degree. All the usual. *Yada, yada.* I felt bad I hadn't pressed her for more details. Not that I wanted any details, and I'd get the *deets* tomorrow, anyway.

Note to self: Ask Mom how's she's really doing.

Before I could reverse out of the lot, a Honda Civic, front-wheel drive, pulled in behind me, and a thin woman with long legs got out. She handed the driver a credit card from her designer handbag, he handed it back, then she shut the door and stared in my direction. She looked like she'd been quite attractive at one time, but that was more than a few years ago. Her blonde hair brushed her shoulders, and she was stylishly dressed in expensive jeans—ones that I happened to know cost about four hundred bucks—a fashionable top, and super-cute lace-up boots. I was busy comparing her boots with my beige high-heeled sandals—beige because I was hoping for a boring, uneventful day—when she walked up to my driver's door and I noticed her eyelash extensions and fake nails.

I buzzed the window down. "Can I help you?"

"I'm here to pick up the Volvo." Her deep frown laid waste whatever beauty she held in my eyes a moment ago.

"The black Volvo T8?" Like I had another Volvo that wasn't black or a T8.

"Yes. I got a call from the police that I could come get it." Her eyes flashed and her chin went up. So she was one of the city's celebrity, entitled types. Oh, goody.

I threw the gear into park and turned off the truck's ignition. My feet hit the ground as I slid down from the cab. I extracted an empty garbage bag from the compartment under my truck bed. "Come with me." I led her back through the locked gate, and she watched as I ripped the yellow police tape from the car and wound it into a ball. I said, "I was here when the police opened up your car."

A dark cloud shifted into her eyes. "Yeah?"

"I know about the money. And the hand." I stuffed the crime scene tape inside the garbage bag.

"I don't know how that hand got in my car. I left the car in the alley because I didn't want to park it on the street." She caressed the paint finish on the hood. "I had no idea it would get towed."

"You didn't see the no-parking sign?"

"I only left it for a minute."

I'd heard all the same excuses before. "Did you go to Main Street Coffee?" Mike Horn, the one who called me to move the Volvo, owned Main Street Coffee, a rival coffee shop to Kristen's.

"No. The art gallery next door."

"Can I get your name and ID, please?" I couldn't release the car to just anyone.

"Courtney Rearden." She extracted her wallet and flipped it open to show me her driver's license. "How much do I owe you?"

"Are you any relation to Rory Rearden?"

"He's my nephew. You know him?"

"He's a friend of mine." I'd towed his vehicle a couple times. He drove a nice car that seemed to break down often. He's a frequent customer at Roasters and a likeable guy with a lopsided grin. An outgoing person who always had a lot to say.

"Can I get a 'friends and family' discount?"

What the hey? She looked like she could pay top dollar. There were times when I gave discounts and even free tows, but I questioned if this should be one of those times. Remember the two bags of money in the back of her car?

I said, "Hold on," and stepped a few feet away. I dragged my cell phone from my pocket and called Rory, who verified that Courtney was indeed his aunt. "She's asking for a discount," I explained.

"Oh man, I'm so sorry, Delaney."

"That's okay. It's just that she doesn't look like she's hurting, if you know what I mean. But I'll give her a good rate since she's your aunt."

"Sure, sure. I do know what you mean, I do know. She can afford it, but she can be funny about money. She's funny like that."

I said in a low voice, "Something weird is going on. You know there were bags of cash found in the backseat of your aunt's car…along with a chopped-off hand?"

"What? No, didn't. I had no idea. No idea at all. Hey, I'm not far from your lot, so wait for me. I'll be right there. Just give me a minute." There was a click and the phone went dead.

To stall for a little time, I swept up the garbage bag, walked it over to the dumpster, slung it inside, and sauntered back, taking a long while to return. Courtney Rearden's fists stabbed into her hips and her lace-up boots tapped the ground, but before she could complain, Rory's Lincoln Aviator, rear-wheel drive, roared into the lot and Rory jumped out. Younger than me by a few years, the guy wore high-end jeans and an untucked button-down. His light hazel eyes and numerous brown freckles were much the same as mine, although the similarities ended there. He had black hair, not red. Lucky him.

"Hey, Rory." I gave him a nod before flicking my gaze over to his aunt. She was really fuming now.

"Where's Uncle Rick? Where is he?" Rory stared at his aunt through slitted eyes. He wasn't smiling today.

She wagged a finger at him. "He's on set. You know that."

"Why are you driving his car? Why aren't you driving your own car? I don't get it."

"I can drive the Volvo if I want."

"What's this about bags of money and a hand?" His voice rose about an octave over normal. "What do you have to say about that?"

"I told this tow truck driver," she sneered at me, "that I know nothing about that hand."

"Hang on a minute. How did a hand get in Uncle Rick's car? How did that happen?"

"Someone put it in there when I left the Volvo in the alley behind Main."

"A hand? Someone put a chopped-off hand in Uncle Rick's car?" He stared at his aunt in disbelief. "You didn't lock up the car? You know Uncle Rick always keeps his car locked. Didn't you lock it?"

"I guess not." She shrugged one shoulder.

I agreed, "That's right. The car was unlocked when I towed it." Who would leave bags of money in an unlocked car?

"I wasn't talking to you." She swung her angry gaze toward me and we exchanged tense looks.

A crease formed on Rory's forehead. "Aunt Courtney, you can't speak to Delaney like that."

"Who's Delaney?"

"Me." I jabbed my thumb into my chest.

"Oh, I thought you were Del. Tell me how much I owe you. I have things to do." She hefted her purse higher on her shoulder.

My face scorched hot. "One hundred sixty dollars." I took her credit card and ran it through the card reader on my phone. After I returned her plastic, she stormed over to the Volvo, tucked her purse then herself inside, and peeled out.

Rory and I just looked at each other. I said, "I charged her full price. I forgot to give her a discount."

"Don't worry about it. No worry at all. Now tell me what this is all about. What happened?"

I gave him the quick version that began with the hand in the duffle bag and ended with, "There were two bags full of fifties and hundreds. It looked like a lot of money."

He gave out a low whistle. His gaze turned inward and he was without words for once.

"Rory, this is suspicious. Why don't you call your uncle and find out what he knows?"

"All right. I'll do that. I'll call him right now." Rory keyed in a number and held the phone to his ear, then punched the cell to disconnect. "The call went to voice mail. This thing with the money is so strange, and the hand, a shock. A real shock."

"Yeah, I know. It was to me, too."

"I think my aunt is hiding something. I'm going to try to find out what."

"Let me know if you do. I'm curious." An unlocked car containing that much money was bizarre. The hand just added to the weirdness.

"I will," he agreed, then climbed back in his Lincoln Aviator and took off.

I trundled my truck down Fifth Street, then jumped on the freeway and pulled the visor down to block out the glaring sun. I chugged up the canyon through pines that scented the air and a breeze that shook the aspen trees. Winter in Colorado caused vehicles to slide into snow drifts, but summer caused vehicles not prepared for high altitude to stall on the side of the road. Now that it's summer, I expected to find some of those stalls.

It wasn't until late afternoon that I spotted a Toyota Camry, front-wheel drive, parked in a turnout with the hood up and a man scratching his head.

I slid the truck in behind the Camry and stepped

down out of the cab. I asked the obvious, "Do you need assistance?" Sometimes people said they didn't, that they had a ride on the way.

"I got a flat." The guy looked sheepish. Men often didn't want to admit they needed a woman to change a tire. Especially a woman like me in my beige, high-heeled sandals with the curly fringe at the ankles.

"No problem. I can do that for you. You know where the spare is kept?"

Thankfully he did know and I didn't have to look it up, because I actually had no idea. Some models hid the spares well. My jack is hydraulic and my lug wrench a cordless electric, so it was a snap to remove the flat and put on the spare, once he'd showed me where it was. "Don't drive far on this tire," I reminded him, before telling him the charge.

He winked at me. "You're the one who found those bags of cash. You must be rolling in money."

My mouth flew open but words wouldn't come out.

He handed me his credit card, and I completed the transaction on my smartphone. I could only stare after him as he closed the hood, pulled into traffic and accelerated out of sight. How did he know that I found the cash? And he believed I helped myself to the money. Blood rushed to my face at the thought.

I jumped in my truck cab and cranked the engine. A few miles later, I had to pull over to a wide shoulder to take a call. Sometimes calls were days apart. Other times they came within minutes of each other. This business is unpredictable and requests for assistance varied. This customer actually needed a tow, and after she gave me her location, I remembered to ask, "What kind of vehicle?"

"Uh, it's a truck. It says Ford on the hood."

I closed my eyes with a sigh. "How big? A Ford F150? 250? 350?"

"I don't know."

"Two or four doors?"

"Two."

Some heavy-duty pickups, like utility vehicles and work trucks, are too large for me to haul, but this airhead was not likely to be driving one of them.

I matched the Ford's location to an address. She was broken down in the exclusive subdivision on the mountainside where all the mansions were built. I'd never been called to tow from there before. I maneuvered up the canyon switchbacks, catching glimpses of bricked castles and palatial country homes behind mature landscaping of spruces, bristlecones, and Rocky Mountain junipers. Flowers from the extensive grounds scented my cab through the open window. I sailed past an RV parked on the other side of a rise while a tall woman in her early twenties wearing a broad yellow hat, a sundress, and flip-flops jumped up and down with her arms flailing. I pumped my brakes and came to a stop.

I leaned out the window. "You the one who called for a tow?"

"That's me."

"You're driving an RV. You said you had a truck." I slammed the door when I got out of the cab.

"It is a truck." She pointed to the hood where it said "Ford." She was correct that the motorhome was on a Ford chassis. The RV was an older model, probably not as lightweight as the newer versions, and had louvered windows and yellow retro stripes on the side panels.

"Where do you want it towed?" I asked, giving up

the argument.

She gave me the address, and although it was less than a mile away, I told her I needed to call for another tower, Tanner Utley, who could handle her heavy motorhome. We chatted while waiting, and I found out her name, Savanah Rivers, and that she was from California.

When Tanner arrived, Savanah took in his six-foot-one frame, dark blond hair, and bright blue eyes, then her gaze roamed over his muscled arms covered in tattoos—a geometric pattern, a bald eagle on a pine tree, music lyrics, and the names Annie and Tate, which I knew were his sister and brother. She looked breathless, and I couldn't blame her because my pulse jumped past speed control into overdrive, too. He was that hot.

"Hello," he greeted her. "I'm Tanner Utley."

She said, "You had me at hello, handsome." Wasn't that a line from a movie? It didn't seem appropriate here, although, I reminded myself, I was thinking the same thing.

He said, "Stand back while I hook up."

"Hook up? Sure." She fluttered her eyelashes.

Tanner gave her an appraising look while I rolled my eyes and huffed out a loud breath. Was I annoyed? Much?

He waved his hands to show us where to wait, so the two of us stood together at the side and admired Tanner's good looks and confident manner while he backed up his flatbed, attached the winch, cranked the RV onto the bed, and chained down the tires.

Savanah gave Tanner a credit card, crowding into his space with her hand on his arm. She was nearly the same height as him and was close enough to get a nose full of the musky aftershave he always wore. He returned her credit card along with his business card, then held open his truck's passenger door for her to get in.

I said to Tanner, "See you later," and slumped into my driver's seat.

Tanner just nodded, but Savanah yelled at me, "*Hasta la vista*, baby." Another movie line, if I'm not mistaken. Tanner swerved away from the curb and they took off.

Instead of cranking the motor, I left the key dangling from the ignition and gazed toward the mountain peaks. My mind drifted to thoughts of Tanner. He's an ambitious, self-made man with a business degree from night school, who built up his towing business from scratch and was singlehandedly raising his younger siblings after his parents both died. Byron had asked Tanner to teach me the towing business—that's how we'd met—and he'd mentored me while I was starting out. Tanner also subcontracted some of his work to me, like the tow-away zones behind Main Street. We'd dated for a while, but Tanner's first priorities were his brother and sister, then his business. I'd never known him to stick with a relationship for long. The twinge in my stomach when I thought about Savanah's flirting was probably jealousy, if I'd admit it. But it was over between the two of us.

Like over-over.

Just like with Ephraim.

And I don't want to talk about it.

Chapter 3

All right, I'll tell you.

I'd only been going out with Sheriff Ephraim Lopez, the hot-blooded Latino with the reputation of being a smooth operator, a little while before I caught him chatting up a statuesque blonde. That's when I told him I didn't want to see him anymore. He had the audacity to act all innocent, like he had no idea what I was talking about. I didn't let that fool me. Can you blame me? Him with a tall blonde? And me, a short redhead?

But I missed him. I missed both Tanner and Ephraim. The two most eligible bachelors in town and I'd dated both of them. Tanner first, then Ephraim until a few weeks ago.

Just as if my thinking of Ephraim could conjure him up, his ringtone went off on my cell.

"Hi, ba—uh, Ephraim." I almost called that stinking cheater "babe!" *Argh*.

"Hello, Delaney. Just phoning to let you know the Volvo's been released and you can return the car to the owner."

"Zach already told me, and Courtney Rearden picked the car up this morning." Did the sheriff really think he needed to let me know? Or was he looking for an excuse to contact me? Was he thinking about me like I was about him?

"Oh," he grunted into the phone. "All right then."

"Zach also said you've taken over the investigation. So, this could involve murder?" In the past, we often discussed his cases. He used to be very forthcoming and appreciated my insight. Would he still? I didn't really want to talk to the rat fink, but I had to if I wanted information, you see.

"Could be either a homicide or a serious bodily injury felony. The crime, if there is one, could include the use of a deadly weapon. So, the sheriff's office was assigned the case and it landed on my desk."

"A deadly weapon?"

"Sure. It took some kind of a sharp instrument to cut off that hand. If it isn't a homicide, this crime could rise to second-degree assault which carries a mandatory five to sixteen year prison sentence."

"When you said, 'if there is a crime,' what do you mean?"

"It's hard to determine at this point whether an act punishable by law was committed. We need to establish just what happened first."

I rubbed the back of my neck. "Like maybe the hand's from a cadaver or an old accident…or…?"

"There wasn't any embalming fluid. The stage of decay was early yet. The hand hadn't even changed color and as far as rigor mortis—"

"—Okay, okay." I was happy the sheriff was sharing so many details, but I still swallowed a nasty taste and put a hand over my mouth. "You think the cash was stolen? That could mean robbery, maybe even armed robbery, right?"

"Ms. Rearden claims the money is hers."

"Really?"

It was her car, or rather her husband's, and she did

look rich, but was the money actually hers if she left her car unlocked? She claimed she didn't know where the hand had come from. Could the bags of bills have been dropped into her backseat along with the hand by a criminal trying to evade the law, and now she wanted to pretend the cash was hers? Weren't we all tempted to grab some of the hundreds and fifties? I didn't want to disparage Rory's aunt, but come on. You were thinking it, too.

"Do you believe her? Couldn't it be stolen?" I asked.

"No locals have reported a robbery or theft in that amount."

"Who carries around that kind of money other than drug dealers? And leaves the car unlocked?" Drug dealers had large amounts of cash. Money, a chopped-off hand. I'd seen those crime shows.

"There could be a legitimate reason for the cash, but we haven't ruled anything out."

"Has the money been on the news already? One of my customers mentioned it."

"There's a news release on the sheriff department's website."

"So, you're the investigating detective." I couldn't help wondering if Ephraim had requested the case because of my connection.

"Yes. You can call me anytime. Since I imagine you won't be able to stop asking questions."

"No, I imagine I won't."

"Be careful, Delaney." His voice sounded troubled and uncertain. "Take care."

"I will."

We disconnected at the same time.

Ephraim didn't tell me not to investigate, maybe

because he hadn't actually decided there was a crime…or maybe because he had some regrets about the blonde. As he should. Whatever. I seemed to have his permission to look into the case, and I knew Rory lived somewhere nearby with his parents, so I clicked on Rory's contact in my phone. The address was only a few blocks away.

I turned the key, rumbled down the street, then took a left at the next intersection, glancing around for traffic. A mansion that looked like a hacienda caught my eye and farther along a gated and turreted castle. This neighborhood was certainly not in my comfort zone. I didn't grow up with this. My stepdad's an attorney in Denver who works in family law and bankruptcy and makes a good living, but nothing at this level. When I knocked on Rory's door would a maid in a uniform ask me to state my business or tell me to leave?

Only one way to find out.

My tow truck with the stiletto logo on the door looked embarrassingly gauche parked on the circular driveway of the red brick country mansion with a peaked roof and enormous windows, but I dredged up some courage and unfastened my seat belt. Maybe I'm not the best tow truck driver in town, but I'm not too bad at digging around for clues. So, I got this, I told myself. And besides, this was Rory's house and he was a friend.

A maid did answer the door, but she was wearing jeans and a tee shirt, not a uniform. I knew she was the maid because her hair was tied up in a scarf, she had a pair of those yellow rubber gloves clutched in one hand, and she introduced herself as the housekeeper. And she did ask what my business was.

"I'm here to see Rory," I explained. I was smiling to

conceal my nervousness.

She peered around me for a glance at my truck. Normally I'm proud of that big ole' hunk of metal. I was living my dream of being my own boss, running my dad's business, and helping people, but right now I didn't feel like I belonged here.

"Step inside and I'll get him," the housekeeper told me.

The interior was as grand as the exterior, with an entry hall inlaid in marble and lit by a fancy cut-glass chandelier. So this is where Rory lived. I reminded myself that Rory's a nice down-to-earth guy. No big deal.

He appeared on the second floor landing, and after bopping down the stairs, he came to a halt in front of me. "Afternoon, Delaney. I'm glad you dropped by. I was going to call you, so it's good you're here." His face creased into that lopsided smile that was almost a laugh.

My discomfort melted away. "You were going to call?"

"Come with me." He led me to a kitchen decorated in a French country style and larger than my apartment. When we were both seated at the white quartz countertop with chunky coffee mugs in front of us, he said, "I found out how much money was in the bags. It was five hundred thousand. Half a mil'."

I gulped some air. "That much?"

"And, get this, nobody's seen Uncle Rick since he was at a neighbor's party on Saturday night. Aunt Courtney says he left for Nevada right after the party, but she didn't talk to him before he left. I haven't talked to him since Saturday, either, now that I think about it."

"Okay. Has she called him to find out if he made it

to Nevada?"

"She says she did call and talk to him, but Delaney, I've been phoning his cell all day. He doesn't pick up so I've left a couple of messages, and he hasn't returned my calls…and he always gets right back to me. Always phones me right back or at least texts. Every time. Except he hasn't this time." His eyebrows bent downward. "I think he's missing."

"Missing?" My jaw dropped. "But your aunt talked to him."

"She says she did, but I don't know, Delaney." He shook his head at me.

"You think she's lying about it?"

"Well," Rory rubbed his chin for a moment, "he's supposed to be on a movie set, but I don't know how to reach anyone out there. I guess I have my doubts."

A movie set? Like in Hollywood? I knew there were plenty of rich and famous movie stars in Spruce Ridge, but I'd never met any of them. Celebrity sightings were rare. "What would your uncle be doing on a movie set? Is he an actor?"

"He's a producer. Haven't you heard of Rick Rearden? He's well known. He produced *Bad Blood Society* and *Mob Lander* and a couple others."

I held up a finger like *hold on a sec*. "Rick Rearden? Where does your family come up with these names? It's as bad as yours, Rory." And I'd never heard of Rick Rearden, but then I barely knew the names of the actors in the latest superhero movies.

"I know." We both laughed, but he laughed louder. Rory always complained about his name. He told me that if you said his name fast three times it sounded like you're trying to talk with a sock in your mouth. *Warwe-*

werewin-warwe-werewin. Rick Rearden was almost as bad.

"Did your aunt go to the party, too?" I asked.

"Yes, but she didn't stay as long. She left before Uncle Rick."

"Where are you going with this? Do you think your uncle had something to do with the money? And the hand?"

"I don't know, maybe, because he's not calling me back. I can't get a hold of him. I really think something's happened to him."

That seemed like a bunch of good reasons to be worried. "Okay, I'm following you."

"So, I went over to the neighbor's, the one who had the party, to ask some questions. I got a list of the last people to see Uncle Rick." He unfolded a piece of paper from his pocket. "The guest list. This will help, won't it? I hope this helps."

I grabbed the page and looked over the names. Many had first names only, no last names. At the bottom of the page, I paused with my coffee cup midway to my mouth. I set the cup back down, placed the list next to it, and stared hard at the final name. One I recognized.

Rory asked, "Delaney, will you help me investigate this? The cops haven't even asked about the party. I checked. They took Aunt Courtney's word that Uncle Rick left town."

I gave him a steady look. "Have you told the police you think he's missing?"

"Aunt Courtney made me promise not to make a stink. She's worried the paparazzi will show up. Or that the investors in Uncle Rick's film will pull out if they get wind of any trouble. She told me to trust her. But something's not right. This is so off base."

"And the hand is way too suspicious, almost more suspicious than the amount of money in the bags, so I agree with you." I looked down in my lap. "Rory, do you think, I mean…er… you don't think the hand…"

He swallowed hard. "That it's Uncle Rick's? What if it is? Please investigate. This is my uncle here. My uncle, Delaney. Family, you know?"

"I get that, but Rory, why are you asking *me* to do this?"

"Because it's what you do. You've solved crimes before. You're good at it. And I can't go to the police because of Aunt Courtney."

I pulled the band from my long braid and raked my fingers through the strands. My dad's unsolved death had turned me into a crusader for justice, a believer in finding the killer and making him pay for the crime. The person who caused Dad's accident was never identified and brought to account. This was my chance to right a wrong. Rory needed some assistance here. And I understood about family. Besides, let's face it, I'd already started to investigate. Rory was right; it's what I do.

"So, will you help me?" he asked in a slightly pleading tone.

"Well, I guess I can try." I lifted the guest list back off the counter. "Can you introduce me to your neighbor? I'd like to ask about these names."

"Why don't I call him right now?" Rory dug his cell from his pocket and keyed in a number. The neighbor must've picked up, because Rory spoke into the phone, "James? Do you have a minute? I have some questions about that guest list you gave me. Just a couple of questions. It won't take long." He nodded his head.

"Okay. See you in a few." He punched the button to end the call. "He'll be right over."

"Okay, good." That was easy enough. While Rory stared down the hall toward the door, I asked, "What do you think your aunt was doing with half a million in her car? She had to give you some kind of a reason for it, didn't she?"

"Yeah." He turned to face me. "She said she was going to deposit the cash in the bank after visiting the art gallery."

"Why would she leave half a million in the car while she went into the art gallery? And leave the car unlocked?"

He dropped his head in agreement. "I know it doesn't make sense."

"Where did she get the money in the first place? All in cash. Is it even hers? Could it be stolen?" I could tell a flush started at my neckline. I was accusing Rory's aunt of a crime.

"It's hers." He made a wafting motion. "Dad told me she pulled some money from her and Uncle Rick's vault. My dad has a key so he knew about it. The money is legit. Can you call Ephraim to help her get it back? Aunt Courtney told me she really needs the money back and the police still have it."

So, the money was hers. At least that's confirmed.

"Who keeps that much money in a vault?" I asked. Rory gave me a look like *who doesn't*, so I asked, "Did she tell your dad what she needed that much cash for?"

"An investment of some sort, but she wouldn't say what." Rory tapped his temple with one finger. "I got it. Maybe she was going to buy a piece of art with the money."

"Those Main Street businesses don't sell stuff like that. They offer paintings by local artists for the tourists. Besides, why would she bring cash? Couldn't she have written a check or used a line of credit or something?"

"Cash transactions are not unusual."

Boy, does this family live in a different world from mine. I'm lucky to pull together a hundred dollars. But maybe half a million was not that much in the scheme of things, at least to the Reardens, since their home was worth several million.

Rory said, "It is weird she would leave the money in the car, though. I agree with you there. She's usually careful about money. This is beyond careless unless she intended to leave it there. Could she have left the money in the car for a reason? On purpose?"

I agreed, "Exactly. And what about the hand? Did she tell you anything more about that?"

"She still says she knows nothing about it. Not about the hand."

We gave each other looks of understanding, like we're both thinking the same thing. Like there's a dead body somewhere missing a hand and it better not be Uncle Rick's.

Rory looked a bit green. "This whole thing is spooky. I'll talk to Aunt Courtney again and try to get more out of her. So, you'll call Ephraim to get the money back? Since you know him, and all?"

"Sure, I can ask," I said.

"And you'll investigate." He wasn't asking me. It was more like he was reassuring himself.

"I still think you should tell the police about your uncle. Can't you talk your aunt into it?"

"She insists Uncle Rick isn't missing. And she

thinks it will delay the return of the money and just muddy the waters, you know, with the investors and all."

I patted his hand. "Maybe she did talk to him, but now he's out of cell range or something, and that's why you haven't reached him. He's probably fine." It wasn't the best lie I ever told.

"I hope so, but I need to know. You'll get to the bottom of this. I know you will."

"I'll try."

The housekeeper bustled into the kitchen. "Rory, Mr. Atkins is at the door."

"Thanks, Theresa." He cast a glance at me. "James is here. Come on." Rory led the way to the front of the house.

The person waiting in the foyer had that high-dollar look preferred by older men—an expensive golf shirt and pressed slacks and boat shoes without socks. His bulbous nose and thinning hair drew my attention to his face.

Rory introduced us. "This is my friend, Delaney Morran."

James said, "Nice to meet you," and I murmured the same. Then he said, "Rory, you wanted to ask me about the party?"

Rory handed him the guest list. "Some of the guests only have first names, not last names. Can you tell us anything about them?"

His gaze traveled down the page. "Not really. They showed up with other people. You know how it is when you throw a party. You just catch the first name, if you're lucky."

"Sure, sure." Rory turned in my direction. "Delaney?" He twitched his head, like *your turn.*

I said to the older man, "Do you remember seeing

Rory's uncle at the party?"

"Of course. Rick was there. So was Courtney, but she didn't stay long."

"Did you notice Rick talking to anyone in particular?"

"What's this about?" His gaze darted between us.

"Um…" I gave my friend a look like, *can-I-tell-him*? Rory gave me a slight nod. "I guess Rick left town right after the party and Rory can't get a hold of him."

Rory said, "That's right. All I get is voice mail. I haven't been able to reach him."

"I'm sure he'll get back to you, Rory. He's probably just busy right now," James told him.

"That's what we're hoping." I motioned toward the guest list James still held. "Lance Palmero was at your party. How do you know him?" Lance's was the name I recognized.

James thrust the paper toward Rory. "I don't know him. I think he came with someone else."

"But you have his full name."

"I just happened to remember it after we were introduced. It stuck in my mind for some reason."

Rory nodded and stared at the paper, while I chewed on my lip wondering what else to say.

"Well, if that's all, I need to get going." James wrenched the door open to leave.

"Thanks for coming over." Rory barely got the words out before James hopped outside onto the porch.

"Talk to you later, Rory, and say hello to your dad." He strode down the driveway and out of sight.

"Well, gosh." I rubbed my palms down my jeans. "He seemed in a rush all at once."

"What can I say? He's a busy man. Real busy." Rory

stepped outside and I followed him.

"What does he do for a living?" I was curious about the kind of jobs people had who could afford to live in this neighborhood.

"He owns a lot of food trucks. You know, like the food trucks outside sporting events and bars that don't serve food."

"Like hotdogs and street tacos?"

"Yeah, but some of his trucks are high-end, like Asian fusion and sushi and tapas. Like, gourmet food. Like that."

"I didn't know you could make that much money in the food truck business." I assumed James' house was a mansion like Rory's parents' since he lived nearby.

"He owns quite a few of the trucks."

"Who knew?"

Rory walked me to my tow truck and gave me a loose hug before I climbed inside. I sat and waited until he returned to the house.

Now I know you aren't going to believe this, that it's just too much of a coincidence and too convenient…that it's not likely for a woman like me who lives in a place like Spruce Ridge, but…the name I recognized? The name James claimed belonged to someone he didn't know? Lance Palmero…

He's a drug-dealing gang member.

Also known as Demented.

And I had his phone number.

I know someone who's in a gang well enough to have his number. Yes, a gang. The Thunder Knuckles gang. I get it. What are the chances? But this is a small town, and Lance and I had crossed paths during a prior murder investigation. Remember, most serious crime involves drugs. But I had to remind myself there could be a simple reason why Lance was at James' party. In a small town you bump into the same people all the time.

Before I could talk myself out of it, I punched in Lance's number with shaky fingers. The man didn't answer, "Hello, this is Lance Palmero, how may I help you?" Or, "Hello, this is Demented," his street name. Or even, "Hello." I would have taken that.

He answered, "Who the *eff* is this?" He was called Demented for a reason.

"Uh…" The word barely came out, low and rough like I had a sore throat, maybe caused by my heart stuck fast in there.

"Who's calling me on this *effing* number?"

I paused to let my heart return to where it belonged, then said, "Delaney Morran, remember me? You told me I could call you."

His manner totally changed. "Delaney! How ya' doing?"

"Good, good." I rubbed the place over my chest.

"I'm glad you called. You need help with something, don't you?"

"How did you know I need help?"

"People like you don't call people like me unless they do."

"It's not drugs." *Oops.* I probably shouldn't have brought that up.

"I didn't think it was about product. What's up?"

Just act cool. I'm cool, I'm cool, I told myself. Did I just lose all my cool points for thinking that? "Did you hear about a severed hand found with some bags of money?"

"No shit? Where?"

I told him, then brought up, "The guy who owned the car with the money in it, and the hand, he was at a party that you went to." I gave him the location of the neighborhood.

"Yeah, I remember that good time. Let me talk to some of the fam. I'll call you back."

"Looking forward to it," I said in my best attempt at bravado.

Chapter 4

Out of curiosity, I went home to look up the hot-shot movie producer, Rick Rearden, on the internet.

There were a number of hits showing his film credits and Academy Award nominations, so I went to a website where a picture of him was posted. I could see the family resemblance. He looked a lot like Rory, with black hair, light hazel eyes, and a lopsided smile, but much older. A second picture farther down the page showed him in mirrored sunglasses and a collared shirt. His smile sported a certain amount of arrogance. His image didn't spark a lot of sympathy, but Rory cared about his uncle, and I couldn't help but worry about the man myself.

Boss, Axle's Rottweiler, pawed my jeans, so I got up from my computer to fill his dinner bowl and give him treats from the biscuit bag. Dusk was hitting the sky as the sun started to dip behind the mountain peaks, and after Boss gulped down his supper, we descended the steps to the parking lot. He frisked around before I returned him to the apartment. Once the Rotty had arranged himself on the couch pillows, I carried my laptop across the landing and knocked on Kristen's door. She swung the door open wide.

"Come on in, Delaney." An apron circled her waist and an oven mitt covered one hand.

Clutching my laptop, I shuffled along after Kris into her living room where Zach was stretched out on her white sofa with black pillows. Her apartment smelled like a bakery, sugary and chocolatey. Her decor was all black and white, and although not my taste, I found it comfortingly familiar. Other than style, our apartments were mirror images, two bedrooms, and one bath. The view from her window was more striking than mine, with the Rocky Mountains covered in green pines. Mine looked out on the parking lot.

"Hey, Zach." I turned from him to ask Kris, "What are you baking? Cookies?"

"Chocolate chip." She bent over the oven to peer through the glass window, then straightened to open the door. "You're just in time for cookies hot out of the oven."

"Yum. I missed dinner and I'm starving." My mouth watered as Kristen slid out the cookie sheet and placed it on a stovetop burner. Zach lowered his stockinged feet to the floor and padded out to the kitchen.

I plopped my laptop on the counter and studied the plate stacked with warm cookies. "Zach, I know the sheriff's department's in charge now, but I have a general question I'm sure you can answer for me."

He gave me a look like he wasn't so sure. "A general question?"

"About police procedure. The police would've identified that hand from its fingerprints, right?" I grabbed one of the golden brown cookies and sank my teeth into the gooey taste of heaven.

"Generally yes, but…"

"But what?" I swallowed and licked my teeth for chocolate.

Kristen looked up from prepping another batch. "The prints were removed from that hand, Delaney. Isn't that right, Zach?"

I nearly dropped my half-eaten cookie. "What? How's that possible?"

"Let's just say generally that prints can be sanded down. But you shouldn't have mentioned that, Kris." Zach gave her a *shush* look.

"Sorry, Zach." Kristen explained to me, "I asked Zach about it, and he told me the victim had not been identified and why."

"Wow." I gave Zach a questioning stare. "That's a clue."

Zach said, "Forget it, Delaney."

"Right." I pressed on anyway. "So, sanded? The prints were sanded off. At least his fingertips weren't chopped off like the hand was." I clapped my fingers over my mouth. Kristen and I gave each other wide-eyed looks. Like *ouch!* A cut-off hand with cut-off fingertips. I'd been thinking of going for another cookie, but drew back.

Zach didn't seem bothered. He snatched a cookie off the plate and popped it in his mouth.

Kristen dropped teaspoons of cookie dough onto the sheet pan. "What about DNA, Zach? The police can make identifications from DNA, that's common knowledge."

"How about it, Zach, just generally, you know." I stared at Zach, waiting for his response, glad his girlfriend was the one asking the question.

He grabbed another cookie. "DNA doesn't help unless it's in the database. Collected DNA samples are entered into a national database called the CODIS, but only from known criminals. Sometimes DNA is on genealogy websites, too, but we don't have the resources or time to track it down. That requires an analysis at a special crime lab that neither the city nor the county has. And it's too expensive to send DNA to the Denver lab for testing. Especially if no crime has been established."

I said, "Okay. So, a DNA analysis hasn't been done on the hand." It could be inferred that the fingerprints would've been in the police database and that's why they were sanded off. Not everyone's fingerprints were on file.

Zach dabbed a napkin to the crumbs in his mustache. "We're getting close to specifics now. That wasn't a general question."

"Here's a *general* question. What other kind of evidence is collected *generally*?"

He alternated his gaze between me and Kristen. "Well, forensic specialists collect all kinds of things, like blood spatter, hairs, carpet fibers, dirt, pollen, and plant debris, if any is available, which I'm not saying any was in this case."

"Okay." Nothing I didn't already know from *CSI*. "So, I was looking up Rory's uncle on the internet."

"Rory's uncle?" Kristen asked, "Why did you look him up?"

"He's the owner of the Volvo, so he's involved in this mystery. Rory told me he's a movie producer." I opened my laptop on the counter and clicked on the page I'd bookmarked. "This is Rick Rearden." They gathered at my screen to look at his picture.

"Who knew Rory was related to a celebrity?" Kris stepped away and slid the filled cookie sheet into the oven, then set the timer.

"You should see where Rory lives. Actually it's his parents' house, a mansion with a housekeeper."

Zach walked back to the couch and lowered himself down. He stuck his feet in the hiking boots he'd kicked off under the table and began to lace them up. "I need to head out, Kris."

"Here, can you drop these off at the women's shelter?" Kris had filled a basket with a couple dozen cookies.

"Sure." He lifted the basket off the counter. "So long, Kris."

My phone dinged with a text message for roadside service for a Subaru Outback. "I've got a tow, so I'm heading out, too." I tucked my laptop under my arm. "See you later."

Zach and I walked out together. "I know you can't tell me anything official, but what do you think happened? You say a crime hasn't been proven, but something criminal had to have happened, don't you think?"

He stopped on the landing. "Of course there was a crime. Was it murder or body mutilation or both? That's what Ephraim will have to figure out. Aren't you glad this has nothing to do with you this time?"

I paused at my apartment door. "But I towed the Volvo. It was in my possession, so it kinda does concern me."

He didn't reply except with a long steady look. "This is serious, and it could be dangerous. There's a criminal offender out there."

"I know, Zach. Really." I gave him a tight smile, then felt his eyes on me as I went into my apartment. Once inside, I dropped off my laptop, patted Boss on the head, grabbed my keys, left a quick note for Axle that I'd fed his dog, then I started on my way.

I turned right off Fifth onto Columbine and took another right onto Main, past the expensive boutiques and the coffee shop that rivaled Kristen's, Main Street Coffee, all closed now, this late at night. The only light was from streetlamps hung with hummingbird feeders and flowering baskets. I left-turned on Washington where the Subaru Outback, all-wheel drive, was stalled with its hood up. The Outback had a California license plate. Mass migration from the Midwest to the Rocky Mountains now included those from the West Coast, too, so it wasn't unusual to see California plates.

A man, perhaps in his thirties, stood by the Subaru. He wore a tee shirt and jeans with oversized sneakers, and he looked like he needed a shave.

I unfastened my seat belt and got out. "I received your text about a tow."

"I can't get it to start."

"Have you had this problem before?"

"Never. She always runs great."

We both stared at the complicated engine under the raised hood. I said, "Did you check for vapor lock?" Vapor lock is a common high altitude problem in the summer.

"What's that?" His vacant, ski-bum look could be the reason he came here from California.

"The fuel injection system plugs up when overheated." I felt like such a professional vehicle recovery agent for knowing this. I actually knew more about engines than my customer. *Yeah-ez*. But considering this vague man, maybe that wasn't such an accomplishment. "Let's check it out." I showed him how to unlock the fuel line by pouring a little cool water from my water bottle over the fuel pump. It worked.

"How much do I owe you?" he asked. After I told him my minimum for roadside, he said, "Are you the one who towed that car with the money bags?"

I clamped my teeth together then released a deep breath. "Yes."

He clutched his wallet to his chest and gave me the silent question stare, but I kept quiet, so he opened his wallet for the cash. While he paid me, I happened to cast a look in his backseat full of camera equipment. "Are you a photographer?" I asked.

"I am." He put his wallet back in his pocket. "Hey, I dig the shoes."

My beige, high-heeled sandals.

A nice compliment.

I'll take it.

"Do you know I'm known as the high-heeled tow truck driver?" I asked with a laugh.

"No, I didn't. I just tapped on the first tow truck driver that came up on my search. I sent you that text through your website." He shoved his phone in his pocket with his wallet.

"Thanks for using me. Please consider leaving a review." I guess some of my business was just down to luck. I'll take that, too.

****

The next morning, the sky was the kind of robin-egg blue only seen at altitude. I relished the smell of the mountains and the fresh pine needles in the crisp summer breeze that made you wish you could fly over the treetops up to the highest peaks. We drove through town with the windows down, Axle and me, each in our own thoughts.

Five minutes after dropping off my roomie, I was

inside Roasters on the Ridge where Mom had arranged to meet me today. My phone rang while I waited for my double espresso. Caller ID showed Lance Palmero. The gangster.

I cleared my throat convulsively. "Good morning, Lance. How are you?"

"I got news. You up for chilling?"

"Sure. What's that mean?" I didn't know any gangster talk and hoped I didn't sound too dense.

"A meeting. At the coffee shop?"

"Roasters? That's where I am right now."

"On my way."

I think I just agreed to hang out with Lance Palmero, a/k/a Demented, but at least the coffee shop's a public place, and Mom wasn't due to arrive for an hour. Hopefully Lance would be gone before Mom walked through the door. I took a breath of the coffee aroma to clear my mind and told myself...*one problem at a time*. What's the worst that can happen? I did suspect Lance sold drugs and quite possibly murdered people, but hey, I was the one who called him. What did I expect? Only to talk on the phone and not in person? Well, yes, I did kinda expect that.

I traversed the dining area, snagged the table in the corner, and let myself get my caffeine-high on. *I could do this. I would do this*, I told myself.

My stomach lurched when Lance entered the shop and gave me a nod, then he strutted up to the counter and ordered a drink. The lightning bolt tattoo on his forehead peeked out from under the brim of his ball cap, and a body piercing in his neck reminded me of a miniature barbell stabbed through his skin, suggesting where he got the nickname, Demented. He was close to my age, maybe a little older, and definitely a lot more streetwise. Once the to-go cup was in his hand, he paid the cashier from a large roll of bills he stuck back into his pocket. He came up to me and set his sugar-free vanilla latte—what baristas called a *why bother*—in the middle of the table.

He said, "You're blazing today."

I said, "Thank you," since it sounded like a compliment. Sure, let's go with that.

He screeched out a chair and took the seat opposite me. "So, this is what I found out. I heard there's a new high roller in town."

"What's that mean?"

"He's living large, you know."

I didn't know, but could make a guess. A guy carrying a lot of money, like Lance did. "Does this have to do with the party?"

"The high roller wasn't there, at least I didn't see him. I'm just truthing the news on the street. You wanted to know what's up and I'm telling you."

"Okay." I turned my espresso cup around and around in my hands, trying to make sense of it. "You know who Rick Rearden is?"

"Sure, sure, the movie guy." He hunched forward resting his arms on the edge of the table.

"Did you see Rick at the party?"

"I saw him go upstairs with a lady. I don't know who she was, but she wasn't his old lady. That woman's a bitch." He said this with a harsh edge. "His old lady, she was yelling at Rick, then she stormed out. It was after she left that Rick went upstairs."

I took a moment to consider the scene. "That's interesting. What were Rick and his wife arguing about?"

"What do dudes argue about with their women?"

I gnawed on my lower lip. "You don't know who the lady was? The one he went upstairs with?"

"Nope. My word is bond. I'm telling you truth." His gaze roved over the restaurant tables. There were two elderly gentlemen playing chess and a couple of teens giggling in the booth by the window.

"And I appreciate the information, Lance." I flashed him a quick smile. There was nothing to fear here after all.

He smiled back at me. "Why don't you call me Demented?"

"Because you don't feel demented to me, you seem quite reasonable, other than your tattoo." I pointed to his forehead and laughed, and he laughed with me, so I relaxed even more. "Do you mind if I call you Lance?"

"Nah, since it's you asking." His grin revealed dazzling white teeth. "You need a nickname, Delaney. What's yours?"

"My mom calls me Laney."

"So, your gang name's Laney?"

I snorted back a laugh. "Gang name? No."

"You need a nickname. How about Del?"

My dad's name. I was happy when my customers called me Del. A lot of them did, since that was the name of my business, Del's Towing. "Sure, I'd like that, but why do I need a nickname?"

"Cause you're an honorary member of the TKs, the Thunder Knuckles Gang."

I tried to keep a shocked expression off my face, but couldn't help the heat flooding my cheeks. "You're kidding, right?"

"No, ma'am." He leaned back in his chair and tucked his thumbs into his pockets.

I'd met Lance last year when I discovered the bullet-ridden body of a member of the Thunder Knuckles Gang in a car on the side of the road. Lance had considered the victim his brother, and when I solved the crime, Lance considered me his friend. I didn't know I was also one of the gang now.

"What's it mean to be an honorary member?"

"It means, I got your back, Del." He shot an imaginary gun. "Pow, pow, pow."

"Excuse me?" I glanced over my shoulder and all around. "Someone might hear you."

"I get it, I get it. Kill the noise. But Del, you need a tattoo." He tapped his head where the dark blue lightning bolt colored his skin. "I know just the place where you can get the ink done."

I said, "Hard to pass up, but no."

"It's part of the gang initiation." He looked disappointed.

"We can talk about it later." Or never.

"I'll call you when I get more of the down and dirty on the new guy. In the meantime, think about that tattoo." He stood up and patted me on the top of my head like I was his little sister or favorite niece. Or his pet. His long legs carried him across the room, but he stopped and gave me the peace sign before he pushed out the door.

In addition to being a high-heeled tow truck driver, I'm now a member of the Thunder Knuckles Gang. Honorary TK member, that is. I cracked my knuckles, no pun intended—Axle would've appreciated that—and checked my bicep muscles, but there weren't any, so I'd better not let it go to my head.

I was a little wired here. I darted into the back room to catch Kristen in her office.

"Lance Palmero just told me I'm an honorary member of his gang." I took a deep breath and reveled in the calming smell of the coffee beans that filled the storeroom shelves.

She pushed her chair back from her desk and brought her eyebrows together. Boxes of organic sugar packets and napkins jam-packed her office and stacks of order forms crowded her desk. A small printer stood in the corner. "Good heavens, you're going to have to explain that."

I told her about my meeting with the gangster.

A frown crept onto Kristen's face, erasing her usual smile. "You need to tell him you don't want to be in a gang. It's not right. Don't associate with criminals, Delaney. Whoever walks with the wise becomes wise, but the companion of fools suffers harm."

That sounded like it might be a bible verse and it was probably good advice, but how could I tell Lance I didn't want to be in his gang? Would he accept that?

"Why did you even meet with him?" she asked me in a low, worried voice.

"He knows Rory's uncle."

Kristen's jaw dropped. "He knows Rory's uncle? The movie producer?"

"Yes, the owner of the car where the money and hand were found."

She shook her head as if stumped. "Why didn't you just tell Ephraim about him and let the sheriff handle it?"

I flushed with self-doubt. She was probably right. But sometimes a criminal is who you need, so I said, "Lance wouldn't have liked me talking to the cops about him. Besides the police know who he is, and they can contact him if they want." The sheriff's office could find out about Lance the same way I did. If they were doing a good job, they'd learn about the party and who was there. They'd find out a new criminal was in town and that Rick had been seen with another woman. And that Rick was missing. I couldn't tell Kris all this, because that would be like telling Zach, and he would grouse about it. As I said, if the police were doing their job properly they would know anyway.

"I know you mean well," Kristen said, obviously determined to be kind, "but I'm worried about you."

She wasn't the only one…

I'm in a gang now. The Thunder Knuckles. The TKs.

That made my stomach feel squishy.

Chapter 5

When Mom walked into the coffee shop, her hair was out of place, like she'd driven with the window down, which she never does, and the preoccupied look in her eyes made my stomach squeeze even tighter.

"Good morning, Laney." She pressed me in a hug.

When she let go, I said, "Hang on, I'll be right back."

I went to the counter for her usual non-fat latte and brought it to the table with a smile. Mom forced me to put on a happy face because I would not admit to my mother that there was anything wrong in my world. She'd go on and on about it if I did. Besides, it was my turn to find out what was happening in her world.

"So, do you have anything to tell me?" I took the seat across from her.

"Why do you ask?"

"You don't seem yourself."

She scooted her chair closer and her face brightened. "I do have a surprise."

"What?"

"I bought a condo in Spruce Ridge. We can see each other all the time."

Get out! I didn't see that coming. I'd nearly fallen off my chair and it took a few seconds to compose myself. "You did what?"

"Bought a condo at the ski resort, about ten minutes

from here. Just think how close I'll be."

"Yeah. Trying to imagine that." I drew my long braid off my neck and twisted the end.

"I figure it's an investment property."

"I see." It was starting to make more sense, and relief flooded my churned-up stomach. "So, you're going to rent it out?"

"Not right away. Will and I had a fight. I've moved out." She held up a set of keys, dangling them in the air with a ringing sound. "I'll be staying in the condo."

I could only look at her with unfocussed eyes and was unable to speak.

She patted my hand. "Nothing for you to worry about. I'll be fine."

I finally gasped out, "What happened?" A wave of sadness constricted my heart.

"It's silly and he'll come around." Her face shuttered. "Really, Laney, please don't be upset."

I blinked away tears that threatened to pop out from behind my lids. Having never warmed up to Will, I was always a tad distant, a childhood habit that was hard to break, so I was surprised that it bothered me so much. I said, "All right, Mom, but you need to tell me about it."

Her mouth tightened. "It was nothing. Nothing at all. I was just passing along some news to Silvia, you know, that nice woman who lives down the street—"

"—Sure, I know who you mean."

"Well…Will got mad at me for no reason. No reason at all." Anger boosted her voice a little in volume. "He had no right to say those things."

"What did he say?"

"He called me a gossip. Can you believe it?"

Of course, I could. I totally could. "No," was what I

said. "What exactly did you tell Silvia?"

She tutted. "Only that one of Will's partners was getting a divorce and leaving the partnership. So, what?"

"Oh, Mom. That might've been confidential."

"That's what Will said." A look of guilt crossed her face.

Note to self: Suck it up. Mom always worried about me like I was fresh out of high school. I could depend on her to be there for me. It was time to pay her back and be the strong one.

What would Kristen say? She always had the right words.

I faced Mom squarely. "You're so right. He'll come around. He loves you too much." I had to believe that. In the past Will only wanted to make Mom happy. I wanted to trust that that was still true.

She got out a small mirror and ran a hand through her hair, smoothing the strands back in place. "Anyway, it'll be fun to buy furniture. There's a store at the mall I want to check out. I'm heading there next. I might as well go now." She stood up abruptly, tossed her mirror in her bag, and snatched her coffee off the table.

I shot out of my chair and gave her a hug. "Let me know if you need help with anything."

"I will." She actually did seem to be handling it well, but her words had been like a punch to my gut. We left the coffee shop together and I watched until her Chevrolet Suburban, rear-wheel drive, went out of sight.

To say I was shocked by Mom and Will's disagreement was putting it mildly. Will seemed harmless, a very average attorney working at a mediocre law firm. He didn't seem like a fighter. He wasn't the curious type and didn't question my occasional requests for legal advice. I suspected he didn't have faith in me or believe that I'd be able to make my business a success without his help. In spite of the little bit of friction between us, I wanted the old folks to get along.

No one wants to rattle the cage that makes the family's structure fall apart. That reminded me I wasn't the only one going through a family drama.

I dialed up Rory. "Did your uncle ever get back to you?"

"No. He's missing, I'm sure of it. Can you come over to my house, Delaney? My aunt's home now. We can ask her some questions together, get her to talk."

"She's home? Your aunt and uncle live with you?" I pictured the red brick, peaked roof mansion with floor to ceiling windows. The house was certainly big enough.

"They stay in the guesthouse when they're in town."

A guesthouse? Of course there was a guesthouse. "Okay, on my way." I rammed my key in the ignition and started her up. Did I care anymore if my red Fulcan Xtruder with the small dent in the front was parked once again in their fancy circular driveway? That's a hard no. I'd gotten over that.

Rory's frame filled the doorway when I climbed up the front stairs. He stepped outside. "Let's go around to the back."

I trooped behind him along a stone pathway that led through mature, lush landscaping with purple sage, orange day lilies, and the sweet blooms of zinnia. We walked the length of the sidewalk until we came to an arched gate. On the other side was a long, rectangular swimming pool, unusual for a mountain town. I bent low to dip a hand in, and the heated water warmed my fingers. Then I jumped up and quickened my pace, my black high-heels slapping the wet cement. Black to match my dark outlook today. A small two-story, red-brick cottage, dwarfed by the mansion but about the size of the house I grew up in, was on the other side of the pool. The white wooden door was flanked by windows. A comfortable looking patio set with blue-striped cushions was to the right of the doorway.

Rory knocked on the screen. "Aunt Courtney, it's Rory."

A curtain twitched at the window. Courtney Rearden pointed a laser stare out at me, then she stepped outside. "Did you get the money?"

Rory looked to me for an answer. I said, "I haven't had a chance to ask the sheriff yet."

"*Humpf.*" She ripped her gaze from me to glare at her nephew.

"Aunt Courtney, let's sit down. We have some questions for you. Just a few questions." He took her elbow and led her to one of the patio chairs. Because the sun was bright in the sky, he opened the red, white, and blue umbrella over the tabletop and angled the pole for shade. He took the seat to the right of his aunt and I sat next to Rory, across from her.

I pressed my hands together and tucked them between my knees. "Rory says he hasn't seen your husband or heard from him, but you don't want to go to the police. Aren't you concerned?"

Her mouth compressed. "When are you going to talk to the sheriff about the money?"

"We'll get to that, Auntie. Tell Delaney what you told me. You know, about the last time you saw Uncle Rick. Tell her." Rory turned toward her with an eager look. "Please, Auntie. Delaney is here to help."

She met my gaze. "You'll ask that sheriff about the money?"

"I will," I promised.

She gave up a sigh. "I was with Rick at James' party across the street. I left around ten and came back here. Rick said he wanted to stay for a while longer. I went to bed around ten thirty and when I woke up, he wasn't there, so I thought he'd taken the jet to Nevada."

"Did he pack his bags?" I asked.

"He keeps an overnight bag on the plane and has clothes in his trailer on the set."

Rory asked, "Did you really talk to Uncle Rick on the phone? Did you really?"

She was silent for seemingly forever, her hand playing with her shirt sleeve, her pulse thumping in her neck. She finally whispered, "No."

"What do you mean, no?" Rory angled his forearms on the edge of the table and leaned in.

"I can't get hold of him either. I talked to his assistant, and she says he hasn't shown up, but I told the police Rick was on a movie set and out of cellphone range."

"Why would you tell them that?" I asked.

"Because of the phone call."

"What phone call?" Rory and I asked at the same time.

She averted her eyes and took a maddeningly slow time to consider the question. A wind kicked up, and the umbrella over the table fluttered in the breeze.

The bags of money. The missing husband. The severed hand. That tumbled around in my brain for a moment or two. "Is this a kidnapping?" I asked. Admit it, you were thinking the same thing.

"Kidnapping!" Rory's eyebrows climbed up his forehead. "Do you believe it could be, Delaney? Kidnapping? Really?"

I gave him an *isn't it obvious* look.

Rory's eyes cut to his aunt. "Auntie?"

"All right, all right. Yes. Rick's been kidnapped." His aunt's breath came out in a shudder. Rory and I exchanged looks, his shocked, mine sympathetic.

"So, the morning after the party, when you realized Rick wasn't home, you assumed he was on the movie set. Then you got a phone call?" I asked her.

"Yes."

I guessed, "A phone call demanding a ransom. You got the money to pay the kidnapper, and that's why the money was in the car. But something went wrong with the drop-off, and when the police asked you about the money, and your husband, you lied and said Rick was in Nevada?" She nodded along with my words. I asked, "Why didn't you just tell the police the truth?"

"Because the kidnapper instructed me not to. And I don't want the story picked up by the media. The paparazzi would start following me and not in a good way. Then, what would happen to Rick? I can't take that chance."

Rory dropped his head to his chest, but I couldn't look away from his aunt.

She continued, "Rick just started filming a new movie and there's a risk the financing could be withdrawn. So let's not tell the police or anybody else, including the family. No one knows but the three of us." She swiveled a finger between me and Rory, then aimed it at herself.

I leaned back and crossed my arms. "Even Rory's

dad? He doesn't know?"

"No." She gave Rory a pleading look. "You can't tell anyone."

"Dad should know about this. I can't keep this kind of secret from him. He should be told. He needs to know. It's his brother we're talking about."

"No." She half rose from her seat.

"It's okay, Auntie. It'll be okay." He patted her arm and she sank back down, then he shot me a warning look.

"So, what went wrong with the drop-off?" I asked her.

"You. That's what went wrong You towed the Volvo before the kidnapper could make the pickup!" Her voice rose and she shot me a condemning glare. "It's your fault Rick is still being held hostage."

Oops.

My bad.

"Does the hand belong to your husband?" I had to ask.

Rory clutched at his aunt's arm. "It's not Uncle Rick's, is it? Is it Uncle Rick's? Is he okay? Do you think he's hurt or…dead?"

Courtney shook her head. "It's not Rick's hand."

"Are you sure?" I studied her face.

"I'd know my own husband's hands. This hand was bigger and the nails dirty and torn. Rick always has nice manicures. Rory, I'm sure it's not Rick's." Her gaze softened on her nephew. Maybe she had a tender side to her after all.

I asked, "What was the hand doing in the bag of money? Where did it come from?" This was too bizarre. The hand had to belong to somebody.

"I said I don't know." Her eyes did a shifty thing.

Could I believe anything she said? Was she telling me a big, fat lie? She lied at first about talking to her husband on the phone. She lied to the police about where her husband is. What whopper was she going to tell next?

I said, "Why did you leave the car in the alley behind Main Street?"

"That's where the kidnapper told me to leave it."

"Was the person who called a man or a woman?"

"The caller used a voice distortion device and told me to get half a million in bills of various denominations, so I got fifties and hundreds. I need that money back so I have it when the kidnapper contacts me again. You'll call the police, right Delaney?"

Rory's aunt was a piece of work. Going to the police would go a long way to figuring this out. Someone concerned about her husband would contact the police. I said, "If you told the sheriff everything, they'd help you. They'd probably return the money to you and find the kidnapper."

"No." Her face had a closed look. "They said 'no police.' "

The pool's heat pump kicked on, emitting a buzzing sound, and the wind made the umbrella billow in and out. The air smelled of chlorine with a hint of coconut sunscreen.

Rory thumped the table. "Wait, back up a sec'. I'm still thinking about the hand. If it's not Uncle Rick's, whose is it? Whose hand is it?"

I tapped the tabletop. "And how do you think the hand got in the bag of money?"

Courtney pursed her lips but didn't answer.

I said, "I did find out the police can't identify the victim from the hand. They don't know whose it is." I left it at that.

"Forget the hand." She stood, cell phone clutched in one fist, then extended the phone and aimed it at her face. She stepped over to the side of the pool, hip out in a glamour pose, and snapped some selfies. Rory and I stared at her while she tapped on her phone. Then she said, "You two, get me the money back. Do it," before stomping to the guesthouse door and wrenching it open. She swept inside, and the door clicked shut behind her.

"That was weird. Did she just post a selfie?" I asked her nephew.

"Yeah. She does that a lot. She has a large social media following, you know, she's an influencer. She makes money at it."

"Hunh." I'd never met an influencer before. I said, "What do you think about this situation with your uncle? Does it have something to do with your aunt and her followers?"

"I don't know, Delaney. My uncle kidnapped! I mean, it's hard to believe that could happen to us."

I didn't find it difficult. The Reardens appeared to be millionaires. His uncle was famous. Courtney was an influencer. *Jussayin*.

We stood and pushed our chairs back under the table. Rory walked me past the pool and out the arched gate. He stopped in the driveway next to my truck to remind me, "Aunt Courtney will never let me go to the police."

"That's crazy, you know." I tugged my keys from my pocket.

"Delaney, you've got to find Uncle Rick. This is a mystery and you're good at solving mysteries. And, please, talk to Lopez about getting my aunt's money back. Maybe if we get it back for her, she'll cooperate and tell us what's really going on. I think she's still not telling us everything."

"I think she's hiding something, too." I beeped my truck unlocked.

"Yes, I'm sure she is."

"She's very insistent about the money. I understand she wants to be ready when the kidnapper calls again. If they call again. But, she seems to care more about the money than anything else."

Rory nodded, his arms crossed over his chest. "I hear ya. I was thinking the same thing. We've got to solve this because I don't want anything to happen to Uncle Rick."

"I'll see what I can find out, but you need to convince your aunt to go to the police." I swung myself up in the cab and plugged the key into the ignition.

"I'll work on her. Promise to do what you can to find him." He stepped aside so I could close the truck door.

"Okay," I promised. Not to help his aunt. Forget that. But to help Rory.

Chapter 6

—We've got to talk. You have a minute now?—

As soon as I punched the send button, I felt a panic moment. *OMG what did I just do?* What will Ephraim think? That I want to get back together? That's often what the *we've got to talk* message is about.

He texted back.

—Yes, we need to talk. Come on by the station. I've always got time for you. —

I jumped out of the truck and paced, flinging my arms around. What to do? What to do? You can't take back a text. But I did need to talk to the sheriff. The kidnapping trumped personal matters. I dialed up Axle.

He answered with a grunt.

I asked, "Where you at?"

"The auto body shop. Why you asking?"

"Can I come get you? I'm in the neighborhood." Everywhere was in the neighborhood in this small town.

"Sure. That'd be fine."

I pulled up and Axle stepped out of the auto bay. He shambled over, then climbed into my passenger seat. "So, what'd you need me for? Don't want to go alone on a tow?" Axle sometimes rode along as my wingman, especially in the middle of the night when I didn't want to go out by myself.

"No, I don't have a tow, but can you go with me to the sheriff's office?" I pulled the truck out onto the road.

"You don't want to be alone with Lopez?" Axle knew me pretty well.

I gave him a slanted look, then shifted my eyes back to the windshield. "Something like that. So, you're not too busy at work to go with me?"

"Nah, I was just sitting around talking to Shannon."

Axle's girlfriend Shannon was Byron Oberly's niece and worked the front desk. The two of them seemed very comfortable together, more like friends than girlfriend-boyfriend. But isn't that the way it's supposed to be? I never managed to achieve that kind of relaxed state. I wonder how Axle and Shannon carried that off?

What the what? I did a mental forehead slap. When I started to look to Axle as an example, I knew I was in trouble.

The Clear Creek County Sheriff's office was located on the highway leading out of town in a modern building with big windows and lots of natural light. The duty clerk escorted us into Ephraim's office. I entered first and the sheriff's face lit up, but then he saw Axle behind me and furrowed his eyebrows. With Axle here, Ephraim would certainly think he got the wrong idea from my text. At least that's what I wanted him to believe…that I didn't mean what he thought I'd meant. I did not want to talk about our relationship. I did not want to ask him about the new girl, the tall blonde he was flirting with at the makeup counter at the mall. What was he doing in the makeup department anyway? Not that I cared.

Did I care? Yes. No. I don't know.

At least having Axle along would throw a cold bucket of water on that conversation.

I slid into one of the visitor's chairs and Axle took the other.

Ephraim Lopez was taller than me by ten inches, older than me by ten years, and had the bronze complexion of his Mexican heritage, with dreamy brown eyes and thick black hair. He always smelled like citrus, jasmine, and musk—clean and fresh and appealing, just the way he looked now. He sat behind his gray metal desk in his sheriff's light blue uniform, and his cowboy hat hung from a hook on the wall.

The mountain town of Spruce Ridge started out as a mining village, then became a tourist destination, a last stop on I-70 before the divide and the ski resorts. In the prior decade it transformed once more, this time into a desirable second-home location for the rich and famous. One could encounter people such as Ephraim wearing cowboy boots, a throwback to the city's western beginnings, as well as out-of-towners and outdoorsy types...and folks like me, a car hauler who wore high heels. See, I fit right in.

Ephraim pressed back in his chair, causing it to squeak. "Delaney, Axle. What can I help you with?"

I forgot why I was there for a minute, but Axle gave my arm a sharp pinch and I untangled my tongue. "I need to talk to you about Courtney Rearden. She'd like to know when her money will be returned to her." See how I handled that? Smooth, if I say so myself.

"Why are you asking for her?"

"She's Rory's aunt. I'm actually asking for Rory Rearden."

Ephraim peered down the hall as if expecting Rory to turn up next. "So, it's Rory is it?"

What did that mean? Did he think I was with Rory now?

I asked, "Can you release the money?"

"The money needs to stay in our custody until our questions are answered. If we determine there's no crime, it will be returned. Why does she need the money back now?"

Axle said, "Everyone needs money…it comes in hand, *amiright*?" Axle laughed at his own joke. "See what I did there? Catch what I said? In hand?"

I felt like tearing his knit cap off and beating him senseless with it, but I said to the sheriff, "It's curious about that hand, huh?"

The sheriff said, "Yes, it is. That's why the money hasn't been released."

"Courtney told me she had no idea how the hand got in her car. What do you think happened?" I scratched my head. "Did she ask you to find out where the hand came from?"

"No, she did not, and you shouldn't be asking me that either, Delaney."

Before I could think of a snarky retort, which I'm usually pretty good at, the duty clerk knocked on Ephraim's open door. "Parker Smith is here for you."

"Have him come on back."

I got up to leave. "Please call Courtney as soon as you release the money. Thanks, Ephraim." Axle trailed after me, dragging his feet, until I said, "You coming?"

A man in a suit and tie passed us in the corridor as we made our way back to the lobby. I gave the man, Parker Smith, a once-over because nobody around here wears a suit and tie.

Once Axle and I were in the parking lot, I asked him, "What's wrong with you?"

"What?"

"That was real mature." I twisted his ear. "Joking

about the hand."

"Ouch!" He batted my fingers away then scrambled into the truck's passenger seat. "I thought it was pretty funny."

"You're delusional."

Once I started up the motor, he said, "I couldn't help notice Lopez didn't give you any of the inside scoop. *Whatsup* with that?"

"I know." This was different from the past when Ephraim shared information with me. "We aren't together anymore. I guess that's why." I dropped the truck into reverse and backed out of the parking space.

"Shouldn't make a difference. You'd think he'd still want to draw on your super power, your intuition."

I nodded at him. "You're so right." I do have intuition. Axle often teased me about being a super sleuth. Ephraim used to ask me my opinions, but not anymore. "Who do you think that man was, the one meeting Ephraim after us?"

"I dunno." He shrugged and began to fiddle with his phone.

I drummed the steering wheel with my fingers, waiting for traffic to clear before turning out of the lot. I said, "Parker Smith."

"Who?"

"His name's Parker Smith." I slammed on the brakes and Axle braced himself on the dash. "I saw his name on the party list." Axle gave me a *whoa* expression. "Let me explain. Rory's uncle went to a party at a neighbor's house and…and…"

"And what?"

"Rory's uncle must've met Parker Smith at the party the night he was *kid*…I mean, a couple nights before I towed the Volvo. That's why Smith was at the sheriff's station. He's some kind of a witness. He must be the same person. Parker isn't a common name."

"But Smith is."

"I'll bet it's him."

Axle bobbed his head up and down. "Probably not a *coinkydink*."

Are the police investigating the same things as I am after all? If so, I'm on the right track. But I almost spilled the beans to Axle about the kidnapping. I'd have to be careful. Courtney was insistent that no one else find out. Axle may be a pain in the ass at times, but he was the closest thing I had to a brother and I usually didn't keep secrets from him.

I let off the brake and sped down the street. After I let my lil' cuz' off at our apartment, I cruised around looking for stalls until it was time to motor over to the alley behind Main Street.

This is the deal with the tow-away zones: Occasionally during daytime hours one of the Main Street business owners called us to remove a vehicle, like Rick Rearden's Volvo, but after closing hours Tanner and I took turns monitoring the loading docks to make sure they were cleared for deliveries. He took three weeknights and I took two; parking was allowed on weekends. Sometimes I removed three or four illegally parked vehicles a night, generating a big piece of my income. When the drivers returned to find their vehicles gone, they figured out pretty quickly they'd been towed, since the "No Parking – Tow-away Zone" sign was a dead giveaway. They'd call the number on the sign, and we'd explain where they could pick up their vehicles at the impound lot. *Easy, peasy*.

A good gig.

Most of the time.

The other times when the drivers were over-the-top angry, it was not so good.

Tonight the tow-away zones remained empty. I was staked out behind a row of dumpsters, blessedly stink-free for once since the garbage had been picked up earlier that day, and I scrolled absently on my cellphone. An engine rumbled in the distance. A minute later a black, one-ton truck with *Tanner Towing* on the door appeared and slid in next to mine. I alighted from my cab, still in my trademark black stilettos, to meet Tanner at our back bumpers. We greeted each other with the usual *what's up* and *not much*.

Tanner propped his behind against my tailgate, his long legs stretched out in front of him, and his feet crossed at the ankles. Goosebumps tingled my skin. He angled his body toward me and I wanted to lean in to him, but restrained myself.

"Savanah called me a couple of times," he said.

"Who?" I wracked my brain for the name. His gaze rested on my fingers combing through my hair and I quickly let go of the strands.

"Savanah. The hippy girl with the RV. I towed her on Chaetae Mountain Drive."

"Of course, I remember her. Did she have more trouble with her motorhome?"

"None that she told me about."

I stared at my black stilettos. "Why'd she call you?" As if I didn't know. Tanner may be a simple car hauler, but he was an attractive man, very successful for a thirty-year old with his own business and fleet of trucks.

"She wants me to go to California with her."

I snapped my head up. "What?"

"She thinks I should be in the movies."

"Really?"

Tanner scratched the close-trimmed whiskers that covered his jaw and upper lip. "Like that would ever happen."

I pretended to study the alley. "It could happen." It's true this six-foot-tall hottie, with dark blond hair and blue eyes, had the handsome looks of a leading man.

Tanner put his hand up to shield his eyes from the sun that was about to dip behind the mountains. The night sky extended out in layers of blue, from a pale, baby-blue to a deep indigo where the peaks met the sunset. He said, "I'd never uproot Annie and Tate. This is their home." Tanner's teenage siblings depended on him, since their parents had both died within a few years of each other.

"Right. You can't go anywhere." I breathed out a little sigh of relief.

He dropped his eyes and shook his head. "No. Are you with Ephraim anymore? I heard you broke up."

"We're taking a break." My heart rate quadrupled, but I reminded myself that I needed to figure out my feelings for Ephraim before letting my attraction to Tanner confuse everything.

He asked, "Are you seeing anyone else?"

I took a quaky breath. "No."

"Well, Laney, a pretty woman like you isn't going to stay single for long." The Hot Tow Man was flirting with me. Was he playing with my emotions? I'd been able to maintain a decent business relationship so far with Tanner, and I didn't want to mess that up. Oh, the romantic drama of it all.

A voice came from the loading zone. "Hey, you two."

Tanner and I both did a one-eighty to gaze at Mike Horn coming out the back door of Main Street Coffee. He tramped down the concrete steps and hastened over. Mike's long hair covered his ears and curled on his shirt collar. His tee shirt and jeans looked like a style worn by men much younger than him, and his broad smile forced his cheeks into round knots. He gave me a *perv* vibe the first time we met, but after I got to know him I realized he's only a man in his forties going through a mid-life crisis.

His eyes sharpened on me. "I heard about all that money you found in that electric car, the Volvo, Delaney."

"*Jeez*, everyone knows. How did you find out? From the news release?"

"Well, there's been a lot of talk in the coffee shop."

I hazarded a guess and asked, "Have you been telling your customers I was mixed up with the money found in that Volvo? Please say you haven't."

He waved away my comment. "I can't help it. It's such an amazing story."

I pulled in a tight breath. "Do you know Courtney Rearden?" When Mike gave me a perplexed look, I said, "She's in her fifties, tall and thin, blonde hair, dresses well."

"Oh, yeah." He nodded. "I know Rick Rearden. Courtney's his wife."

"How do you know Rick?"

Tanner tapped my elbow. "What's going on?"

I told him, "It was Rick's Volvo."

Mike let out a low whistle. "I didn't realize it was

his."

I did a palm up gesture. "The reason I'm asking is, did you see Courtney that day? She was the one driving the car."

"No. I wasn't paying close attention. I only noticed the car because it was in my loading zone."

"You didn't recognize Rick's Volvo?"

"No. I don't know what he drives. I don't know him that well. He comes into the coffee shop, that's all."

A four-door Acura, front-wheel drive, swerved into the alley, but kept going through to the next block. We all watched the sedan until it merged into traffic. No way a driver would try to park here with two tow trucks standing by.

Mike inclined his head toward the coffee shop's rear door. "Gotta get back inside. Talk to you later." He scaled the concrete stairs and disappeared into the building.

I turned to say something to Tanner, but he was halfway to his truck.

"I'll see you later, Laney. I got a text for a tow." He waggled his cell at me before yanking open his driver's door and swinging up inside. His truck sped over the gravel, leaving me alone in the dusty alley with the empty dumpsters. The sounds of a group of pedestrians on the sidewalk and accelerating cars on the street carried back to the alley. Live music started up from the direction of the brewery next to the coffee shop. They must have hired a band to play tonight.

A Mustang, rear-wheel drive, pulled in, so I revved my engine, and when I caught the driver's attention I inclined my head toward the "no-parking" sign. The Mustang left, and a Toyota Avalon, front-wheel drive, rolled in, saw me, and keep going. I decided to cruise the length of the alley, and by the time I returned, there were four illegally parked cars blocking the brewery's loading dock. They weren't leaving. They were staying for the show. Needless to say, I got busy after that.

Right before the parking restriction ended at nine, I cruised down the alley one last time. Axle, with a bunch of his buddies, cut through on foot.

I buzzed down my window. "Hey, Axle."

"I thought I'd run into you." Axle waved goodbye to his friends and climbed into my passenger seat. "You might as well give me a ride home."

I grabbed his tee shirt with the name of the indie band, *Badflower*, in my fist, pulled him closer to me, and sniffed. My nose twitched with the up-close musky smell. "Have you been smoking weed, Ax?" I shoved him away.

Axle sniffed, smoothing out his shirt. "Are you *fricking* kidding me? I smell like this cause everyone else was smoking. I only had a couple of brews."

I stared at him, wanting to believe him. "But you're underage!" He was eighteen.

"So what? It's just beer. Man, you sound old."

That took me down a notch. I put my truck into gear and let off the brake. "I do, don't I? Sorry. You went to see the band?"

"Yeah. They were okay. You must've been hard at it tonight. We had to park five blocks away to find a spot."

"Good thing you did or your friend would've been towed."

"I told them that." He popped his earbuds in and tapped his knees to the music.

Once I exchanged the truck for the Fiat and we cruised back to our apartment, I parked, flicked the headlights off, and we bailed out of the car. Walking up the stairs, I received a call. A Chevrolet Caprice, rear-wheel drive, needed a tow. I turned around to head back down, but Axle stopped me with a hand on my arm.

"I might as well come with you." He was still stoked from the band, bobbing his head to the music in his earphones a little more vigorously than usual.

"Thanks. Wish I hadn't already dropped off the truck." It was going on ten, not late but dark with a full moon and slight breeze. I was always a little intimidated by the night because I'm a daytime, sunshiny kind of gal.

When the two of us showed up with my Fulcan self-loader, a man was wiping the Caprice's trunk with a cloth diaper. I've heard of proud owners doing that before, but never saw such a thing until now. And the 1990 Caprice had been modified to a lowrider.

"These old cars need a lot of babying," he explained. "She started having an engine knock, so I pulled over. Don't want to take any chances." He asked for a tow to his home.

With a whine of the hydraulics, my truck's T-shaped bar lowered to the ground. The crossbar extended and the claws rotated around the old lowrider's rear tires. But Axle stopped me from raising the boom. "There might not be enough clearance and you could damage the bumper."

"You might be right."

We both got out and trundled the tow dollies over to the car's front wheels. Once the dollies were strapped in place, Axle pumped the dollies to lift the front wheels, then I hit the button on the remote to raise the back wheels. Another swish and hiss and the target vehicle rose high enough off the ground. We were ready.

"You need a ride, correct?" I asked my customer. Sometimes vehicle owners were picked up by somebody, but in this case the man was alone.

He passed his credit card over to me. "Do you mind?"

"Of course not. I'd be happy to give you a lift." When I tucked the remote back in the cab, I said, only so Axle could hear me, "Can you get in the back? I don't like my customers to sit behind me. It's not safe."

"If you say so." Axle snorted, obviously with a sense of small town security. But there was nothing wrong with being cautious.

The man asked me, "Are you the tow driver who found all that money?"

The hair on my arms stood up on alert. Did he want to rob me? I looked at Axle in my rearview mirror but he wasn't paying attention. I told the man, "I didn't take any of it." He looked like he didn't believe me. Darn that Mike Horn for spreading rumors. My grip tightened on the steering wheel, and I kept throwing glances at the passenger until we arrived at his house.

After dropping off the lowrider and heading home, I sang out, "Lowrider in the sky."

The teen shook his head. "Now who's tripping. It's ghost rider, not lowrider."

"What's a ghost rider? I like lowrider." I hummed the tune.

"I heard that."

"I sang a little softer, "Lowrider in the sky. Yippie I oh, yippie I aye."

He fiddled with his phone and pretended not to hear

me the rest of the way home. I live to bother Axle.

I dreamt that night of Tanner getting ready to tow an RV to California. First he winched the motorhome up onto one flatbed, then he said he needed a bigger car hauler and moved the RV to another flatbed. Then, when he tied down the wheels he couldn't get the D-rings on the lift straps to tighten, and when he was ready to pull out, he was suddenly back to winching the RV onto a flatbed again. It was one of those quest-dreams that took all night to resolve. When he finally drove out of sight, a feeling of sadness came over me, a deep regret like someone had died, and I woke up. The sun had not yet risen.

Axle's Rottweiler, Boss, must've heard me stir, because he padded into my room and jumped on the end of my bed. I patted the pillow next to me and he bellied his way up. I scrunched the top of his head and went back to sleep.

I woke up later than usual and hopped in the shower. I'd just gotten out when I heard a knock on the door. After throwing on my robe, I went to answer it.

"Morning, Laney." Mom stepped over the threshold with a plastic cake container in her hands. She set it on the counter.

"Want some coffee?" I asked.

"Of course." She reached up to the cupboard at the same time I did, but beat me to the coffee mugs. She filled one and handed it to me, then filled the other. "Sit down, Laney, and let's visit for a while."

"You don't have to wait on me, Mom."

"What would you like for dinner? I'm baking several casseroles and freezing them. I'll bring you over one."

Giving up, I dropped my elbows to the table and covered my eyes with my fingers. "Anything you make is great." I took a gulp from my mug for a caffeine infusion. "How's everything going? Have you talked to Will?"

"No." Her lips thinned. "Why aren't you dressed? You feeling okay?" She looked about ready to rest her palm on my forehead.

"I'm fine, all fine." The last thing I needed was a mother hovering over me with a thermometer and a bowl of soup. "Actually, I need to get ready to head out soon."

"Me, too." She rose from her chair and emptied her cup in the sink, then washed it and set it on the drainer. "I'll be back with that casserole, Laney. Have a good day."

"You, too." I gave her a quick hug and release before she left. I clutched the top of my head. What was I going to do about my mom?

Axle waltzed into the kitchen. "She gone?"

"Yes. Where's your cojones?"

"Hey, I was just giving you some mother-daughter time." He glanced over my shoulder. "Oh my God!"

"What?" My breath caught.

"There's a cake." He swooped down and popped the lid off in one fluid motion. "Want a piece?"

"No. Well, sure." It would go great with coffee.

"I heard about the casseroles," he said around a full mouth, crumbs falling onto his shirt. "When do you think she'll bring those over?"

"Any moment." I looked toward the door and so did Axle. He licked his lips and swallowed like he was salivating, then slid past me and dashed toward his room. "I don't need a ride today. I got my Altima running again." He was always taking it apart and putting it back together to "increase its performance."

"Okay," I said to his retreating back, then shoved a last bite of cake in my mouth.

He left the apartment before me, so I stopped at Roasters on the Ridge on my way out. I was waiting in line for my usual espresso when Rory Rearden walked in. Right behind him was Savanah. That woman! Tanner had spent the night towing her RV. Of course, that was only in my dream, I hoped.

"I'm glad to bump into you, Delaney. This is convenient. I have someone you need to meet. You'll want to talk to this lady." Rory swept his arm to the side. "This is Savanah Rivers. She was at my neighbor's party."

My eyes went to the girl who caused me a sleepless night. A premonition or a nightmare or both?

She asked, "Yo, Adrian, you remember me?"

I said to her, "My name's Delaney."

"That's a line from a movie." Her voice was laced with distain.

Rory glanced between us. "You've already met? You know each other?"

I answered, "Savanah called me for a tow the other day. In fact, she was in your neighborhood."

"I know. That's how we ran into each other, isn't it, Savanah? I saw your motorhome and asked you about it."

"That's right." Her gaze skimmed over the room. "Where's that hot tow truck driver you were with?"

I tried to keep an irritated look off my face. "Probably busy working." My turn came up in line so I placed my order and lingered to the side.

Savanah told the barista, "I'll have what she's having," then she laughed at her own joke. "No, actually, I'll have an iced coffee." After we skirted around the tables to the pickup counter, Savanah said to me, "I heard how you towed that Volvo with the money in it."

"You and everybody else. And I didn't take any of the cash."

"A fake hand was in the car, too?"

I said, "It wasn't fake. Why do you think it was fake?"

Her eyes went wide and her cheeks blanched. "I just assumed it wasn't real, I guess. I thought it must be fake." She made a face. "*Ick*. Houston, we have a problem."

"It was the real deal. So, Savanah, about the party you were at, did you see anything suspicious?" I might as well question this witness who was at the place the kidnapped victim was last seen.

"Like what?"

"Drugs?"

"Of course drugs were there…*duh*…it was a party." She rolled her eyes. "No big deal."

"Do you know Rory's uncle? Rick Rearden?"

"Sure, I know Rick. I've met him before."

I was in luck. This woman could provide essential information. "Did you see Rick at the party with a woman?"

"Yeah."

"And?" I waited while her eyes darted around. "Can you describe her?"

"I can do better than that, I know her name."

I enthused, "Really?" The barista, Guy, called out our drink orders, and we plucked them off the counter. I asked him, "Is Kristen in her office?"

"No, she left on an errand. She'll be back in a bit."

"Okay, tell her I stopped by, would you please?" I twisted toward Savanah. "Let's grab a table." I led her and Rory to my favorite spot at the window. "So, who was the woman?"

"Courtnee Clyborne, spelled real cute, C-o-u-r-t-n-e-e. Savanah's not my real name, either. It's Vanna Sue. Can you believe it?" She took a sloppy draw of her iced coffee. "Courtnee's most famous movies are *Dead or Not* and *Dead or Not Revisited*."

I gave Rory a puzzled look, like *are you following this?* Rory said, "That's Aunt Courtney's stage name. Clyborne is her maiden name."

"Yeah, Courtnee Clyborne is Courtney Rearden, Rick's wife. She was the one with him at the party." Savanah said this with a serious face.

"Of course Rick was with his wife." I tried to keep the exasperation out of my voice. "Tell me something I don't already know."

"Well," she huffed.

"What, no movie-quote comeback?" I massaged my temples, wondering if I was going to get anything useful out of her. Rory caught my eye and shrugged.

We both turned our attention to Savanah, but she stood as if to leave. She said, "Tell Tanner hi from me," and walked out the door.

What a ditz. And she was interested in Tanner, that much was obvious.

Right now I'd be glad for someone to tow her all the way to California. Someone other than Tanner, of course.

Chapter 7

I connected with Main, turned west, and drove up the entrance ramp to I-70 to scout for orange-tagged stalls marked by the city for removal. The highway split Spruce Ridge, with mansions climbing the forested south slope and shopping centers sprawled in the narrow valley below the north slope. Soon the town was behind me, and my truck labored to climb the elevation. With both windows rolled down, the dry scent of hundreds of pines blew in. The side of the road progressed from pines to sagebrush to barren landscape above tree line, but remained clear of stalls. At the top of the pass, I got off to turn around and return the way I'd come. A gray Ford Fusion hybrid, front-wheel drive, exited behind me and reentered the expressway after me. I did a double-take because I swear a gray Fusion had gotten on the highway where I'd entered from downtown.

I swerved off at the next exit that went into the Park-N-Ride where commuters picked up a bus to Denver. I extracted myself from the truck, and my pulse revved up a notch when the gray Fusion glided up next to me, and a man in a suit and tie climbed out. I recognized him, Parker Smith. He'd met with Ephraim right after Axle and I stopped by to talk to the sheriff. His name was on the party list, so he was there along with everyone else in town, I'd come to believe, since both Savanah and Lance had been there, too.

"Why are you following me?" I crossed my arms and tucked my fists under my elbows.

"I need to talk to you." His short brown hair was cut in a close-cropped style and his suit matched his vehicle, gray.

"About what?"

He slid his hand in his jacket and came out with a badge. "I'm Parker Smith with the Denver Drug Task Force."

I leaned in to examine the badge and it appeared legit. I straightened back up. "Okay?"

He took a step closer. "I have some pictures I'd like to show you. Have you seen any of these men?" He handed me a short stack of photos.

After shuffling through them, I answered, "No, I don't recognize anyone." I was glad Lance Palmero wasn't among them, and that I didn't need to lie to protect a fellow gang member—honorary gang member, that is. I gave the photos back to the drug agent. "Why are you showing these to me?"

"I thought one or two of them might've been in the vicinity of the Volvo T8 that you towed."

"Oh." I gave him a curt shake of the head. "No, I didn't see anyone around the car. Did the money in the backseat have to do with drugs? Are those photos of drug dealers?" I knew, or thought I knew, that the money was a kidnap ransom, but this agent must think there was a drug connection.

"I'm just checking everything out." He pinched one of the photos between a finger and thumb and held it up. "You sure you didn't see this guy?" The picture showed a nice-looking man with dark eyes and hair, but he had bad teeth with a couple missing in front.

"Yes, I'm sure I've never seen him before. Does he have a name?"

"Iceman." Parker Smith seemed disappointed. "A nickname because he ices people, as in kills them. He's dangerous and you need to contact me if you see him." He passed me his business card.

I stuffed the card in my pocket. "You were at the party with Rick Rearden, the party at James Atkins' house?"

His eyebrows drew in a fierce scowl. "How did you know that?"

"I saw the guest list, and the name Parker was on there, an unusual name." I eyed him with suspicion. "Were you undercover?"

"I went there with someone else. I'd rather you didn't mention it to anyone."

"You were undercover. You shouldn't've used your real name. Or is Smith even your real name?" I was sure now that it wasn't and gave a throaty laugh, but Parker set his jaw in a hard line. "Is that where you saw Iceman?" I asked.

He tapped his knuckles on the Fusion's metal hood. "Call me if you see him."

"I will." I got back in my truck, buckled up, and tried to loosen the tension in my shoulders. I wondered if he had other business cards with various aliases.

Parker observed me as I ground the gears to get back on I-70. His gray Fusion accompanied my truck for a couple of miles until the Fusion disappeared at one of the exits. My hands still clenched the wheel, but after a few moments they began to uncurl. I quit the highway at Spruce Ridge and headed for Oberly Motors. Once I pulled the keys from the ignition, I phoned Lance

Palmero.

"Who is Iceman?" I asked when he picked up.

"He's the one I was telling you about, the new high roller. He's trying to take over the territory."

"Was Iceman at James Atkins' party?" I turned my back to the open bay outside my driver's window for a little privacy.

"I never saw him there, like I told you before, but I wondered if he was around."

"Was Rick Rearden a drug user?"

"Yeah, he was up on it. Iceman probably was chillin' there even if I didn't see him. I seen Iceman a couple of other times around the parties in those hills."

"In that same neighborhood?"

"Yes, that's truth."

"Do you think Iceman had something to do with the money and the severed hand?" Could Iceman be the kidnapper? That dismembered hand could be Rick's, even if his wife didn't believe it, if Iceman was a killer like Parker said. Maybe not only a killer, but a kidnapper, too, and if so, Rick was surely dead.

"I don't know yet, but I'm asking around."

"Okay, thanks."

"Hey, if Iceman bothers you, I'll call him out. You let me know."

"No hurting anybody, right?"

He chuckled, then there was nothing after that but his breathing.

"Please phone me when you have news." I hit the end-call button on my cell and did a quick over the shoulder. Byron was at his giant red toolbox inside the first bay with noise-cancelling ear protectors covering his ears. Axle, in painter's pants and safety glasses, operated a paint sprayer in the third bay. The garage sounded busy, with the shrill whine of machines and a boom of something heavy hitting the ground.

I decided to check in with Byron, but waited outside the auto bay until he turned around so I didn't startle him.

After a minute or two, he looked over, his eyes widened, and he unhooked his earmuffs. "Delaney, I didn't know you were here."

"Hi, Old Man." I scooted under the open, overhead door.

"Whatcha' doin'? You takin' a break from car haulin'?"

"Yeah. You have a minute?"

"Course I do. Take a seat." He snared one of the rickety folding chairs and dusted off the seat for me. Then he went and got his own. Axle glanced up, but kept working two bays over.

I asked him, "Remember Lance Palmero? That Thunder Knuckles gang member? He's come into Roasters on the Ridge a couple of times."

"He the one with the metal piercin' in his neck? Has a lightnin' bolt tattooed on his forehead?"

"Yup, that's him."

"What about 'im?" Byron wiped his red shop rag down his face and around his neck. Byron is an ex-convict and recovering alcoholic, who was given a job and a second chance by my father. He'd served time for killing a man in bar fight. It was manslaughter because the other guy started the fight, but Byron had punched him and he went down, hitting his head and dying the next day. After Byron was released from prison, he turned his life around and purchased my dad's auto body shop. I was proud of him for making good with his life.

I was also indebted to him for helping me solve a murder last year. That's how we both knew Lance Palmero.

"Lance and I met yesterday. He's sorta helping me out with something."

With a big intake of breath, Byron seemed to swell up. His shoulders rose to his ears, his fingers clenched, and he sat up straight. "Don't tell me you have anythin' to do with that gangster."

I seemed to have two ex-felons who wanted to protect me. Lance and Byron. I rubbed his arm. "Nothing to worry about, Old Man. It's all good. Lance is not threatening me or anything like that. I was the one who called him, and only for information about the money and the hand in that Volvo." I inclined my head toward the open door. "The one I towed over here."

He stared at me in disbelief. It was hard for me to believe, too, that a cutthroat gangster like Demented would prove to be safe, even sympathetic and caring.

"Don't tell anybody I said he was helping me, he may not like it." I made a duck face with flat lips.

"I should say not." His eyes still held concern.

No way I'd tell the Old Man I was an honorary member of the gang. Or that Lance would eliminate anyone he thought was my enemy…unless I could stop him first. Byron would go ballistic if he knew.

"Enough about me. How are you doing, Byron? You okay?"

"Sure, sure. Nothin' new goin' on with me." He narrowed his eyes, not letting go of his worry.

"Your niece doing okay, too?"

"Shannon's fine." His face softened and he visibly relaxed. "She's not here right now 'cause she's in her accounting class." She'd just started her first year of college.

Axle sauntered over from the mechanic's work space to ask, "What's up?"

"Just checking in with the Old Man." I gave Byron a wink. "Hey, have either of you heard of an actress called Courtnee Clyborne? She's one and the same as Courtney Rearden, the owner of that Volvo. The car with the money in it. And the hand."

"Wow, really?" Axle perked up.

"You know who she is?"

"Nah. An actress, though?" He looked starry-eyed, like a fan.

"She's Rory's aunt and old enough to be your mother, Ax. Put your tongue back in your mouth."

"Oh." He shoved his hands deeper in his pockets.

Scratching the back of his neck, Byron said, "I don't know her, either."

"All right, then." I dusted my hands together. "I'd better get back to work. Places to be. Cars to haul." I gave Byron a side hug and Axle a whack to the shoulder before heading out the door.

I flopped back against the truck seat and let out a whoosh of air. I probably shouldn't have mentioned Lance to the Old Man, who was on the over-protective side. That was close.

Maybe it'd be better if I left Byron out of the loop from now on. That made me feel like I was hanging out there on my own, but I was used to taking care of myself. I competed with the all-male tow truck drivers in town. I recovered repos from angry owners. I equipped myself with pepper spray, what's in every female vehicle recovery agent's pocket. I'd even solved a few murder mysteries. So…I got this. My voice within scoffed at this, but I disregarded it. I cranked the engine over and took off.

I received a call to respond to an accident on the mountain pass. After I brought in a light-weight Toyota Tacoma, rear-wheel drive, and I was on my way over to the hamburger stand for lunch, Courtney Rearden called on my cell.

I thought she'd ask about the return of the ransom money, but instead she asked, "Can you pick me up at Rory's house? Actually, I'm a block away from there. I'm at the corner of Annelid and Chaetae Mountain Drive."

"Sure. Give me fifteen minutes."

Looking for the Volvo on Annelid Boulevard, I spotted Courtney leaning up against a stop sign with a ball cap low on her head and colossal sunglasses covering her face. Her jeans were baggy and plain, and her shoes black, flat lace-ups. She was just full of surprises.

I leaned out the window. "Where's your car?"

"Back at the house. I need a ride to town."

"Don't you need a tow?"

"No, I don't need a tow. Just a ride." She glanced up and down the street with her shoulders hunched up around her ears.

I bristled. "I'm not an Uber."

"No kidding. I'd have to pay an Uber." She wasn't even pretending to be nice.

My face flushed hot. "I don't give free rides around town, either."

She tugged her cap lower over her face. "I don't need a ride *around* town, just *into* town. That's all I need."

"That's all?" She didn't catch the sarcasm, so I sighed heavily and reached over to push the passenger door open from inside. When she jumped in, I asked, "Why'd you call me?" Didn't she have any friends who could give her a lift? *Jeez.*

She snapped on her seatbelt. "The paparazzi might notice an Uber, but they'd never suspect I'd leave in this monstrosity."

I stiffened my spine, but kept my voice calm, using the practiced civility I adopted when dealing with customers. "Should I be insulted?"

"Why would you be insulted? You get to help me avoid bad press. Lucky you. Hey, drop me off at Main Street Coffee." She waved a hand, urging me to drive on.

I guided my truck through the labyrinth of cul-de-sacs and dead-ends leading out of the well-to-do community. "I heard that Rick liked to party with some known drug dealers." *Heh, heh.* I can dish the attitude, too.

She said in a snit, "Rumors and lies. Just the kind of fake news those tabloids like to spread."

I gave her a sidelong glance. "Courtney, you can't deny he was at a party with drug dealers. Admit it, you were there, too."

"Rick was not involved in drugs or the party scene whatsoever." She stared out the window.

I struggled not to let her annoy me. "I'm only trying to help you find your husband. If you don't think drugs are involved, we can move on. So, did you have an argument with Rick before you left the party?'

"No, I did not. Who said that?"

"Someone told me about it." Lance was the one who mentioned it. He said Courtney was a bitch and he was right about that. Probably he was right about a lot of things. I stopped at the light on Main Street, and when the opportunity came, I turned right on the red and pulled into the stream of traffic.

"Who was it? What did they say?"

"That you yelled at your husband, then stormed out. He was seen with another woman after you left."

"More lies." She crossed her arms.

Okay. Different approach. "So, you're in the movies, too?"

"Yes, you didn't know that?" Her angry glare bounced off me.

"You went by the name, Courtnee Clyborne."

"So, you're familiar with my work." She got out her cell phone and bared her teeth at the screen.

"Are you going to take another selfie?"

Her eyes flicked over to me and back at the camera lens. "Are you kidding? Not in this truck." She made teeth-sucking noises as she picked something from her front tooth, then thrust her phone back into her purse. "I need that money back for the kidnapper. What did the sheriff say when you asked him for it?"

"He's still trying to determine if a crime's been committed, and he's not going to release the money until he figures it out. You need to tell him about the kidnapping, especially if you want that money back."

"Not going to happen."

"How did you explain to Rory's dad why you needed the money? Rory told me his dad was aware you'd taken the cash from the vault." I weaseled my big truck into a parking space in front of Main Street Coffee.

"I told him that I had an investment opportunity. When I get Rick home, I'll tell the family what the money was really for. Right now, I can't have too many people knowing." She ripped open the door and hurtled from the cab. She turned back, her angry eyes drilling into me. "Tell the sheriff I need that money." She banged the door shut.

I poked my head out the window. "Do you want the money for the kidnapper or for yourself?"

"For the kidnapper, of course." She jogged the few steps to the coffee shop, then looked in all directions before ducking through the door.

Most people who are worried about a kidnapped family member would get the police involved, or better yet the FBI, don't you think? But this was out of my wheelhouse. Maybe the family members of kidnapped victims don't always call in the big guns. Maybe Courtney's behavior wasn't suspicious. What did I know? *Nada. Nuffin. Jackshit.*

I inched away from the curb and pulled a U-turn. I may not know were Courtney was coming from, but I knew exactly where I was going next.

I parked in the lot at the Clear Creek County Sheriff's office, my truck taking up two spaces, but I didn't get out. I squeezed my eyes shut and tried to pull myself together.

Should I just go ahead and tell the sheriff what I knew? That Rick Rearden had been kidnapped? That would be doing my duty as a citizen. But I *had* made a promise to Rory to keep the kidnapping to myself. So, should I simply go in and ask for the money back, like Courtney wanted me to? But I *was* still mad at Ephraim. A slow boil simmered through my blood when I thought of him flirting with that blonde. Some women didn't care if their boyfriend hit on other women, but I cared. It was probably father-abandonment issues, if I was honest with myself.

I thought of another option…should I get the hell out of here?

A knock sounded on my window, almost sending me through the roof.

Chapter 8

"Hi, Ephraim. I was about ready to come in and ask for you." I was at eye level with the sheriff since I was sitting in this high truck cab and he was standing tall to the ground on the other side of my window.

"It didn't look that way to me. It looked like you were debating something with yourself." He skirted the front of the truck and came around to the passenger side, then grappled with the door handle until I remembered to release the lock. He folded himself into the seat next to me, his long legs taking up all the space.

"You wanted to talk?" He tipped his cowboy hat back.

"I just dropped off Courtney Rearden. She asked me to check with you again about the money."

His eyes combed over me. "What's going on, Delaney?"

"I don't know." That was a fact. I was in a total fog.

"You usually have some theory about the crime."

"Courtney is hiding something, I'm not sure what it is." She was hiding more than just the kidnapping, so as Lance would say…I'm telling truth.

He nodded. "Maybe you could explain something else to me then. What's going on between us."

"Uh…" This was *super awk*.

I'd really cared for him when we were going out, but I always knew our relationship was never going to last.

Ephraim was a player. He'd worked his way through most of the single women in town before we dated. He'd seemed to come on to me, but never asked me out. I was the one who called him for a date. I had no trouble making the first move, but I couldn't help wondering if he was really interested. Was I his choice or was he mine? Did he just fall into the relationship because I made it easy for him?

I knew what it was like to luck into things in life. Choices are sometimes made for you, like when I inherited the tow truck. That bit of luck worked out well for me. But the day I came upon Ephraim at the mall chatting up the attractive blonde, I knew I had to end it before he did.

And if he wanted me back, he was going to have to pursue me. I was worth it.

There was also the matter of Tanner Utley, the hot tow man. There was something that drew us together, even though he spent most of his energy on his job and his brother and sister. He'd never move to California because of them. And maybe a little bit because of me?

That I was attracted to both men was confusing. Ephraim wasn't entirely to blame for the breakup. I must not want to commit either.

And I didn't want to have this conversation. Not now.

Procrastinate, much?

I said, "I wanted to ask about Parker Smith. He stopped me the other day and showed me some photos of drug dealers. He wanted to know if I saw any of them around the Volvo before I towed it. I told him I didn't. Are you two working together?"

"We always cooperate with the Denver Drug Task

Force."

"You think that money is drug money?"

His forehead ridged with frown lines. "It's a possibility."

Now was my opportunity to set him right, but I remembered the promise I'd made to Rory, and held back. I asked, "So, you're not going to release the money anytime soon? You're keeping it for evidence?"

"Looks that way." He took a deep breath, stretching his uniform across his chest, providing me with a whiff of his jasmine aftershave, and his scent flooded my senses. His uniform and those cowboy boots looked good on him, too. Not that I was looking, mind you.

To mask the flash of heat that shot through my entire body, I turned the key in the ignition. "I'll tell Courtney."

His gaze held a question but he said, "All right, Delaney." He unpacked himself from my cab and strode back inside the sheriff's office.

I put the truck in gear, but before taking the exit, I hauled out my cell phone to let Courtney know I'd tried again. She wouldn't appreciate it, but I fulfilled my part and wanted nothing more to do with her. From now on, I'd just deal with Rory. He's the one I wanted to help anyway.

Courtney picked up on the second ring. "Delaney. Come and get me right now. The kidnapper made contact."

"What?" My high-heel slipped off the brake and I had to jam it back on.

"Hurry."

"Are you still at Main Street Coffee?"

"Where else would I be?" The phone connection went dead.

"Of course you're still there because you didn't call me for another ride," I muttered to myself. I should ignore her like I'd decided to do, and I took a moment to consider it, but my curiosity was too great. What can I say? I needed to know what the kidnapper had told her.

When I pulled up, Courtney bolted out of the coffee shop at a run. She hopped inside, clutched the dash, and ordered, "We need to get home fast. Let's go!"

I stepped on the gas. "What happened?"

Courtney swung her body around to look out the back window. "That photographer is following me."

I glanced in the rearview mirror. A Subaru Outback, all-wheel drive with California plates, was tight to my bumper. "I recognize that guy." I could see his vacant, ski-bum look from here.

Surprise registered on her face. "You know Wyatt Tagert?"

"I helped him with vapor lock." I hadn't known his name until now, since he'd paid in cash and not by credit card.

"Does everyone in this town have car problems?"

"Everybody's car breaks down at one time or another, especially here. Altitude is hard on engines, and cars often stall on our mountain roads."

"Can't you lose him or get rid of him? Don't you know some maneuvers?"

I drove a couple blocks down Main, and left-turned onto Fifth, the Subaru following along. So, I cranked the wheel, nearly throwing the truck into a skid, and shoved the gear into park. I slammed the door closed with a thud and marched my red platform heels back to the Subaru. I was glad I'd put on my red shoes today, red for power. "You need roadside service?" I asked the man whose eyes dilated in fear. His cameras with the big lenses rested within reach on the passenger seat.

"No."

"Well, since you've been following me, Wyatt, I figured you must need some help."

"No."

"You sure? Because it really looked like you wanted my attention, the way you were following me." I gave him the *what-the-hell* bad ass tow driver glare.

A muscle jumped in his cheek. "I wasn't following you. I'm turning at the next block."

"All right, then."

Wyatt crept his car around my truck, then hurtled the Subaru down the road and took the next corner with a loud squeal.

I tucked myself back inside the truck cab. "All taken care of."

"Good." She expelled her breath with a huff. "I hate those tabloid photographers. They make me look bad. I'm in charge of my own narrative, not them. Besides, I don't want them to make money off photos of me. *I* monetize my own photos."

"By being an influencer?"

"That's right. Do you follow me?"

"No doubt." What I meant was, *no, definitely not*. I asked one more time, "So, the kidnapper made contact?"

"I'll tell you when we get home." Courtney wouldn't say another word, so I swerved into Rory's parent's circular brick driveway in record time.

As soon as we alighted from the truck, Rory dashed out the front door. "Come with me. Come on. Come on." He trotted around the corner of the mansion and we followed at his heels. The three of us jogged all the way back to the guesthouse by the pool. Sitting on the patio table was a brown cardboard box with the flaps open. "Look inside. You've got to see this. You won't believe it! Look! Look!"

Courtney advanced toward the package on shaky legs. She jammed her oversized sunglasses on top of her ball cap, took one glance inside, and her face turned white.

"What is it?" I craned my neck around to peer past her.

"It's a foot." Her voice sounded faint.

"A foot?" I yelped, a hand over my heart. Courtney had on a *you-heard-me-right* expression, but I shoved her aside to see for myself. There it was, somebody's chopped-off foot, torn skin around the ankle, black with old, caked blood. I gagged a little in the back of my throat and almost stroked out.

"Was there a message with this?" Courtney gave Rory a questioning squint.

He shook his head side to side. "Go ahead and check."

I couldn't believe it when she reached in and nudged the foot aside. Better her than me. I had the heebie-jeebies, chicken that I am.

"Nothing." She pulled out a chair and sat down hard. "Maybe the foot is Rick's. I don't recognize the foot, but maybe it's his. I can't tell like I could the hand. I'm sure all feet don't look the same, and if it was bony or fat or something, I could probably tell if it was his. But this just looks like an average foot. It could be Rick's."

I considered that for a moment. "What about the size? Is the foot the same size as Rick's?"

Her head jerked up. "Go get one of his shoes, Rory."

"All right. I'll get a shoe. I'll be right back." He vanished through the door while Courtney and I stared at each other. Her hands tensed and relaxed repeatedly and high spots of color appeared on her cheeks.

"The kidnapper is sending a message. Rick's life is in danger and I need that money more than ever. I need that money, Delaney." Her hands settled into fists and her frown deepened.

"I just came from the sheriff's office. I asked Ephraim like you wanted me to, but the Sheriff's Department isn't releasing the money yet."

Her face hardened and a penetrating, almost evil look, shown out from her eyes.

A disturbing idea crossed my mind. Was it possible she was in on it?

What if Courtney had arranged for the discovery of the severed hand and foot herself? What if she planned the kidnapping of her husband and used that as a ruse to appropriate cash out of the vault? She acted out the scene of leaving the money bags at a drop-off, went inside the art gallery so she would be witnessed, but I'd towed the vehicle before she could make the money disappear into her own offshore account. She must've been shocked when she returned and the Volvo was gone and the cops were involved. She wouldn't want the kidnapping to be investigated until her little scheme was all done and over with and Rick out of the way. Now she wants that money back pronto, or it would all be for nothing.

She continued to scowl. "What in the world is taking Rory so long?"

"I don't know." I had my sympathy-face on, hoping to conceal my suspicion.

Rory emerged from the house with two cross-trainers. "I'm so rattled I forgot if the foot is left or right. Which is it? Is it the right one like the hand? Or the left?"

"The right." Courtney snagged the correct shoe from Rory's hands. She lifted the foot from the box and tried to stuff it in the shoe but it wouldn't go. Courtney said, "Get another shoe. We only need a right one, and bring a pair of thin socks, too." When Rory rushed back inside, she said, as if for my benefit, "Maybe a sock will help the foot slide in."

Blood whooshed in my ears and I was too queasy to speak.

When Rory got back and placed a thin argyle sock in her hand and a black penny loafer on the table, she drew the sock over the hacked-off foot. She stood with the severed foot between her own two feet and leaned over to make another attempt to fit the foot into a shoe, first the trainer, then the loafer. The loafer worked.

The foot was propped upright, covered in a stylish, patterned sock and a classic, penny loafer, looking like the foot of a mannequin clothed for a business meeting or dinner out at a fancy restaurant. Except for the torn and blackened skin just below where the calf should've been.

Courtney slapped a palm to her face. "It fits."

Rory went wild-eyed. "Poor Uncle Rick. Oh my God, poor Uncle Rick. Is he dead? He's dead, isn't he?" He staggered around, running a hand through his hair, tangling the black strands.

His words left me shaken, too. "Maybe it's not your uncle's. Courtney doesn't think the hand is his, and a lot of men wear the same size shoe."

Rory stopped and looked at me with hope in his eyes.

Then I had to add, "We need to call the police and let them figure this out, people."

I imagined what the sheriffs would say when they found the foot dressed up for a night on the town. What would Axle say when he found out about it? I can hear the jokes now. *You need to put your foot down, don't be de-feeted, or did you get off on the wrong foot?*

"No police!" Courtney practically shouted.

"What should we do? What should we do?" Rory's returned panic made his voice reach a high note.

"Sit down, Rory." I led him to a patio chair, where he collapsed, transfixed with horror, and I turned on his aunt. "Why was there a severed hand in the bag of money? Where did the hand come from? Out with it, Courtney."

"The hand?"

"Yes, the hand. If we can figure out where the hand came from, we'll have a better idea about this foot. You haven't told us the whole story. What are you hiding?"

She picked up the pair of trainers from the table and stooped down to set them together on the cement patio, then she sat back up and swiped her sunglasses from her head, folding them in her fidgety hands. Avoidance if I ever saw it.

Rory gave her a pleading look. "Aunt Courtney, please tell us everything you know. There's more to this, isn't there? You have to tell us."

"All right. All right." Courtney threw her sunglasses across the table and they skidded off the other end, falling to the cement with a crash. "The hand showed up here right after I got the first call. Right here." She tapped the glass tabletop with a plastic fingernail. Rory and I both pushed back. "I figured they were sending me a message. But I knew it wasn't Rick's hand, and I didn't want it here, and I didn't know what to do with it, so I put it in the bag with the money."

I covered my lips with my fingers, fighting giggles bordering on hysteria. She tried to give the hand back to the kidnapper? What would they have done when they opened the bag and found the hand inside? I guess it served them right if they got a shock. Or would they even get a shock out of it?

We all stared at the table top. I pictured the hand laying there, all by itself, not attached to anything. No arm. No body. Like a Halloween decoration. Ugh.

Courtney's false eyelashes fluttered. "I couldn't keep the hand in my possession. I didn't want to be caught with it. What if the press found out? Can you imagine the story? It'd be all over the tabloids. Anyway, the kidnapper was just trying to scare me. The hand had nothing to do with Rick or me, and I needed to get rid of it."

"You should've called the police the first time this happened." I gestured toward the foot.

"The kidnapper told me not to, remember? I was trying to do this on my own." She stared off, as if thinking hard.

I grabbed her sleeve to emphasize the gravity of the situation. "You need to take this foot to the police."

She shook her head hard. "No. I won't. I'm afraid of what's going to come next. The kidnapper must be getting desperate for the next drop-off to be a success."

Rory knocked his chair back as he stood. "I'll put the foot on ice. That's what we should do. Keep the evidence preserved for the police. When the time comes, when this is all over, we'll give it to the cops to figure out."

I sent him a mental thank you of appreciation. At least someone other than me wanted the police involved.

"I need that money. The sheriff's got to give it back to me. Delaney, tell them there's no crime here, that the money should be returned." Courtney's words blasted out as loud as a car horn and her eyes were popping.

"I can't do that. It's not true, and I'm not going to lie for you anymore. Ephraim is already suspicious about me asking for the money back." I was getting loud, myself.

Rory bounced glances between the two of us. "Whoa, whoa, settle down, both of you. I'll be right back. Don't fight while I'm gone. No arguing." He returned inside the guesthouse and emerged with an oversized, clear plastic bag.

Courtney removed the sock and shoe and placed the foot in the bag while Rory and I watched. A shiver went up my spine. I could understand a little bit why she returned the hand. Who wants a severed body part in the house?

I said, "You'd better hang on to the box. The police will want it when you get around to telling them. Don't touch the box more than you can help it."

I took a moment to study Courtney. The woman looked white and her eyes were so wide her eyelash extensions touched her eyebrows. A moment ago, I thought I read a foul look behind her eyes, but now I read the fear, and my sympathy gene finally kicked in at last.

I touched her shoulder and gave it a light squeeze. "Are you holding up okay, Courtney?"

She slithered out from under my hand, ruining the moment. "I'll call you when I need another ride." She carried the box and heavy baggie into the guesthouse, to put the foot in the freezer, I supposed.

The whole thing about the hand and foot made me doubt Courtney could be the kidnapper. Where would she get dismembered body parts? Unless they did belong to her husband, and he was dead, and she hacked him up herself. But to what purpose?

I looked at Rory for a clue and he looked as confused as I felt. "What now?" I tugged on my braid.

"I guess we wait for the next drop-off instructions. Please don't go to the police, Delaney. I'm hoping against all odds that the hand and foot are not Uncle Rick's. If he's alive, we need to do everything we can to get him home safely. We have to do it Aunt Courtney's way. You see that, right? You see that, don't you?"

"No, I don't. This is crazy."

"You promised to help me. I don't think I can go on without you. I need your word." Rory's Adam's apple bobbed up and down.

I inhaled the dusty pine scent of cedar tinged with the astringent smell of the swimming pool. "This sucks, Rory."

"So, you understand?"

I swatted the air. "Yeah, yeah, got it." How could I tell Ephraim the truth, anyway? He'd know I'd held back information from the start. It felt too late to do anything about it now.

Then I sensed a presence behind me.

I did a slow one-eighty…and looked right into Rick Rearden's eyes.

Chapter 9

"This is my dad, Randy Rearden," Rory explained.

I blinked a couple of times. Rory's dad looked a lot like the picture I'd seen of his brother, Rick, with dark hair and light hazel eyes crinkled at the corners. He was dressed in business casual, a golf shirt and pants, and black penny loafers identical to Rick's.

He extended his hand, and I clasped it in mine. "Nice to meet you, Mr. Rearden." I sneaked a look at Rory, and he gave me a sideways glance but kept his mouth buttoned up.

Mr. Rearden's grip tightened around my hand as he returned the handshake. "Call me Randy." He sized me up, then said to his son, "Are you busy? That conference call starts in ten minutes."

Rory had told me he was an acquisition manager for his dad's company. That sounded like an important job. I figured they must be working out of a home office today.

"I was just about to head inside." Rory took a few steps, then paused, his eyebrows arched up. "Are we good here, Delaney? All good?"

Before I could answer, his dad said, "Let's go, then."

I stepped aside to let them pass, then went for my truck. As I turned out of Rory's driveway, I spotted James Atkins across the street. I waved, but he acted like he didn't know me, and when I pulled to a stop, he trotted up a long, curved driveway and disappeared around a bend of trees.

My stomach growled as I mounted the stairs to my apartment. You'd think after all I'd heard and seen I wouldn't have an appetite, but I'd skipped lunch and noon was a long time ago. The thought of Mom's cake on the counter made my mouth water. When I reached the top of the landing, Kristen's apartment door opened and my friend stepped outside.

She held two large pizza boxes stacked on top of each other, the cardboard oozing with grease spots. I closed my eyes and breathed in, and my mind flooded with the smells of tomato sauce, garlic, and pepperoni. I rubbed my stomach and said, "Tell me you have some of that left."

She said over her shoulder, "Zach, she's home."

Her boyfriend appeared at her shoulder. "I'm glad you're here. Kris was making me wait for you before she'd let me have any pizza."

"We got it from a new place in town, Joseph's Pizzeria." Kristen chuckled with deep satisfaction. She liked to support locally owned businesses like hers.

"Thanks, you two. Follow me." I worked the key in my apartment door and pushed it open.

The sounds of gunshots, *boom, pop-pop-pop, ka-blam*, filled the apartment, and I stumbled-halted in the doorway, the pizza boxes stabbing me in the back.

Kristen said from behind me, "What's going on?"

Axle was slouched on the couch, a video game controller in his hands, and Lance Palmero sat next to him with another controller. Boss's welcoming bark joined the electronic sound effects.

"Lance?" I didn't think anything more could

surprise me today, but I was wrong.

Kristen brushed past me to set the warm boxes on the kitchen counter. "Pizza delivery," she sang out.

Zach said, "I'm glad we got two extra-large." He opened the silverware drawer and seized a handful of forks. Kris opened the cabinet where I kept the plates. I just stood there, rooted to the spot, my breath caught in my throat.

"Did you say pizza?" Axle asked. "There's beer in the fridge, too."

I swallowed a couple of times. "Lance, what are you doing here?" I gave him my best *what-the-hell* stink eye. Didn't anyone else notice his lightning bolt tattoo and metal piercings? Am I the only one who thought his presence alarming?

Kristen gave me a questioning look. "Do you know Axle's friend?" Evidently the scary-looking man made sense to Kris. I'm surprised she didn't remember he was with the TKs gang, since he'd been to her coffee shop. But Kris was often in the back working in her office.

"Lance Palmero," I mouthed. She raised her eyebrows in a silent question and gave me a slight shake of her head. I leaned closer to her ear. "Demented."

"Oh! Dear Lord!" Her eyes widened.

With my flat palms patting the air, I motioned for her to lower her voice. We had a policeman with us. The last thing I wanted was a confrontation.

Her eyes swiveled to Lance. Maybe she did remember him now, but she must've gotten my *keep-it-quiet* message because she said to Zach, "Don't forget napkins."

Lance said, "Hey, I know you. You're a Five O."

Zach gave him what passed for a cop as a smile.

"Yes, I'm with Spruce Ridge Police. Have we met?"

"Nope." Lance turned his back to us and resumed play.

Zach shrugged, then carried the plates, forks, and napkins to the table. I noticed the cake container was empty. Axle and Lance snagged beers and half the slices from the first box and went back to the couch while the rest of us sat around the table. Boss padded over and plopped at my feet, drool forming at his mouth, and I was finally able to draw a deep breath.

"So, what have you two been up to?" I gave Boss a wedge of pizza, trying to keep my eyes from darting to the video game players. Kris and Zach told me about a new program at their church, something about a youth revival, but I could hardly listen, my mind was traveling in so many different directions, and I had half an ear on Lance and Axle's conversation.

Kris asked me, "So, how about you?"

My attention returned to my friend. "What about me?" I selected another piece of pizza for myself and gave Boss a corner.

"What have you been doing with yourself? Busy with work?"

I murmured a low *hmmmmm*, my mouth full. After I finished chewing, I asked, "Zach, can someone be identified from a foot, like they can from fingerprints on a hand?"

His gaze hardened. "Where'd that question come from? What's going on?"

"Just a general question. I'm curious if another body part would be easier to test or whatever?"

"Like a foot? Not likely."

"So, no then?" I took another bite.

"Well, you can get some information, but usually only race, sex, approximate height, whether the person is in fairly good shape, that kind of thing. You can get prints from toes, but those usually aren't on file anywhere. You can get DNA, of course, but that has to be on file, too. Does this have to do with that hand?"

"Not really." I remembered toe prints counted among the evidence in a prior murder case, then I caught a glimpse of Lance staring at me with hooded eyes, so I changed the subject. "You still coaching youth softball?"

"Yeah." Zach went on about the church league, and once the pizza was demolished and the beer cans crushed in the recycle bin, the couple got up to leave.

I said, "Thanks for giving up your Friday night to spend with me."

Kris squeezed my hand. "We had fun." She cast a glance over her shoulder. "You know what to do."

"I'll talk to him."

"I know you'll take care of this." Kristen always believed in me, even when I doubted myself.

As soon as the door closed on them, I spun around. "Okay, what's going on? Axle, do you know who you're playing video games with?"

"Sure, it's Demented. He competes in video tournaments, Delaney. He won the Champion Cup." Axle had awe in his voice.

"Keep up here. He's with the Thunder Knuckles Gang." It was all I could do not to give Axle a whack on the head. Don't think I didn't consider it.

"Hey, now, Del. Sounds like you're dissin' me." Lance chuckled.

"Can I talk to you outside, Lance?" I jerked my head toward the door.

He got up and patted the top of Axle's knit cap, then sprang forward to open the door for me. He allowed me to proceed him down the steps.

When we both reached the parking lot, I whipped around to face him. "Did you come by to tell me something?"

"I found out Iceman's enforcer likes to cut off hands." He poked a cigarette in his mouth, but didn't light it.

My stomach did a flip. "So, Iceman did this."

"I didn't say that, but it could of been him. That's all I'm saying. Be careful, Iceman may be looking for retribution because you turned that money over to the cops."

"It's not my fault the police confiscated the money. So, Iceman's involved?"

"Alls I know, Iceman's trying to hold down the territory. Any bags of money turn up, he's going to lay claim to. And his MO is to cut off hands." The cigarette stuck to his lower lip and bobbed when he spoke.

"Are you going to light that?"

"I'm trying to quit because I heard smoking's bad for your lungs."

"Everyone knows that from birth."

"Well, I don't want to die from lung cancer."

I glanced at the scar on his upper arm and the healed cuts on his hands, likely from knife wounds. This was getting *way* dangerous. Messing with gang members and kidnappers and drug dealers was playing with fire. Like that's ever stopped me before.

"Someone delivered a severed foot to Rory's aunt."

"No kidding?" He didn't even flinch.

"What should we do?" I asked.

"I got an idea. I know where Iceman chills out. Come with me."

"No way." I did a palms up.

"You got something better to do?" He started down the steps two at a time.

I ran after him. "Well, no." Unfortunately. And it's a Friday night, too. That added an extra layer of *depressing*. "Where are you going?" I couldn't picture a gang-ridden neighborhood in this upscale town, but felt my heart clench anyway.

"No worries. I'm your protection. You'll be safe with me 'cause I'm strapped." He patted a place under his arm where I suspected he had a gun holster or maybe a knife. "My word is bond. I'm telling you truth."

"No killing. No stabbing. No icing anyone?" I can't believe I was considering this.

"Right. Let's jet. We'll take my ride." He indicated a dented, black Jeep with a cloth top.

My skin tingled like a cool puff of wind traveled up my arms and the back of my neck, and my throat was as parched as the high desert, but I managed to cough out, "This'll be safe, right?"

"You're with me. You can't be safer 'en that." He pushed me toward the car. I leaned into him to resist, but he palmed my head in his big hand and caused me to duck down inside the Jeep. He came around to the driver's side. "Come on. Buckle up. We don't move till you do."

Dutifully, I clicked the seatbelt around my middle and sent Axle a quick text that I was running an errand and would be right back. Lance steered us over to the cowboy bar on the edge of town, a known hangout for people who wanted to purchase illegal drugs. Not to honk my own horn, but I'd been here before. I survived it then, I'll survive it now. Piece of cake, I said to myself.

We entered the door to country western songs playing on the speakers. Inside were a lone pool table, an empty dance floor surrounded by wooden tables, and a long, scratched bar, all of which had seen better days. I scooted up to a bar stool and Lance took the one next to me. He ordered two shots, but I changed mine to beer on tap.

Lance said, "This could be your initiation, Del. How about getting that tattoo after this?"

I gulped my beer, wishing to be anywhere else.

A man in worn-out jeans and a once-white tee shirt sidled up to the counter and started a low conversation with Lance. It appeared like he might work on a building construction site or maybe a road crew by the looks of his work boots. I kept darting glances their way, hoping to catch some words, and stared at their rough hands, but they were talking low and I didn't see any hand-to-hand exchange. A few men in denim shirts and cowboy boots came through the door with a couple of jeans-clad women, and they headed directly for the pool table. Someone turned up the music, and the voices of the customers rose a decibel or two. The workman slid off his stool and wandered back to his table where another man, a dude with long, shaggy hair, joined him.

"What was that about?" I asked the gangster next to me.

"Nothin'." He played with another unlit cigarette in his hand.

"I thought you said Iceman hangs out here." I gave Lance a pointed look. No one remotely resembling the man in the photo with the bad teeth was in this bar.

Lance glanced around and shrugged, and we sat in silence for a while more. I was nursing my second beer when he excused himself to go to the restroom.

My phone dinged with a text from Axle.

—where you at?—

I replied that I would be home soon, but I wondered when we'd get out of here because Lance was taking a long time. Was he still in the men's room? Did he slip out to the back alley to conduct some business there? Where was he?

The construction worker remained at the table with the shaggy-haired dude, so Lance wasn't meeting up with either of them in the john or the alley. I studied everyone else, but it didn't seem like any other customers were missing. The cowboy and cowgirl pool players were all at their game. The man at the end of the bar hadn't moved.

I was about to head down the narrow hallway to knock on the door to the little boys' room when three sheriff's deputies burst through the front door and another came running in from the back emergency exit, tripping the alarm.

I whipped around, ready to break into a run, when Ephraim banged through the entryway next.

Busted!

Chapter 10

The pool players dropped their cues on the table with a clatter. The construction worker made a break for the barroom door, but was blocked by one of the sheriffs. Lance materialized from the hallway with his hands deep in his pockets, and his eyes searched me out. When his gaze landed on me, he gave me an emotionless stare.

One of the blue uniforms braced his feet apart and laid his hand on his duty belt. "Stay where you are. Freeze."

Ephraim pushed through the other officers. He barely broke stride, zeroing in on me. I opened my mouth to defend myself, but my throat convulsed. Lance sprinted across the floor and got in between us, his hands fisted at his sides.

Ephraim asked me, "You know this guy?"

Lance answered him, "She's with me."

"Hold on." Ephraim stared down the gangster. "Say that again."

"We came in together," I tried to explain. Dammit if I didn't feel my cheeks go red.

"I see." Ephraim's jaw tightened as he glowered at Lance. "I was going to let you leave, Delaney, but you'll both need to be questioned now."

I gave Lance a stern face as if to say *see what you've done?*

We reclaimed our barstools and waited as two

sheriffs worked their way through the small number of people inside the bar. The first officer was a solid-looking man with a wrinkled face, and the other barrel-chested and stocky. I sucked in my breath when they escorted the construction worker out the door. Had Lance met up with him or anyone else in the men's john for a drug deal after all? Was Ephraim about to arrest Lance, and me, too, as an accomplice since we're together?

Yikes.

The barrel-chested sheriff returned and asked Lance and me to follow him. The two of us squeezed into the back of the sheriff's cruiser and my heart seized up like a motor run dry. We were transported across town to the station, and I was left to sit in the lobby while Lance was taken through the security door, probably to an interrogation room. Parker Smith strolled through the lobby next, looking like a man on a mission, but didn't give me a glance as he proceeded into the secured area. After a long fifteen minutes, Ephraim came out front and guided me down the hall into his office.

"What's this all about?" I helped myself to the visitor's chair.

He sat at his desk across from me so we were facing each other. "We made an undercover drug buy on the premises and arrested the person involved."

My eyes hit the ground. "Lance Palmero?"

"No, it wasn't him. We had no justification for a frisk, so we only questioned him and let him go."

I glanced up to see Ephraim's frown. Lance must not have been dealing. Not tonight, anyway. "Was it the construction worker?"

The sheriff's eyebrows shot up. "You know him,

too?"

"No." Phones rang and footsteps sounded outside his office. I rearranged myself in my seat and cleared my throat. "Why did you bring me in?"

"To put the fear of God in you. What were you doing with a man like Lance Palmero?" His eyes latched onto mine, and he stretched his hand across the desk toward my fingers, as if afraid I wouldn't welcome his touch. I held my breath and my insides quaked, my stomach flip-flopping with uncertainty. Should I tell him everything? Rush back into his strong and protective arms? I could picture myself in his embrace, his jasmine aftershave filling my senses, his arms pulling me closer and causing butterflies in my stomach.

Blushing, I dragged my gaze away from his and pulled my hand back. Where had those thoughts come from? Did he guess what I was thinking?

I asked, "Have you decided when you're going to release that money to Courtney Rearden?"

He slid his hand back, too, and he looked disappointed. He said in a tight voice, "No."

"Have you determined if a crime was committed?"

"Not involving Ms. Rearden."

I slumped back and chewed on a thumb nail. "So, you have no reason to retain that money."

"I don't know how you're involved in all this, Delaney, but I know you are. Lance Palmero is not someone you want to associate with." Disapproval threaded through his words. "Have you found out something you want to tell me about?"

"Not really." Truth, as Lance would say. I didn't know much other than the fact Rick was kidnapped, and I'd promised not to tell the police about that. Was Iceman involved? Were any of my other suspects guilty? I had no solid facts. I wasn't getting very far in my investigation. It was confusing and I had nothing definite to give him.

His intense look said he was worried, but he shoved his chair back into the wall and got to his feet. I skulked along the hallway behind him until he deposited me in the lobby.

Outside in the parking lot, I found Lance leaning against the building. He was on his feet and moving toward me in an instant. "You okay?" He brushed a few stray hairs away from my face.

"Sure. Does this count as my initiation?" I put on my brightest smile as I tried for a joke.

"This was a trip, but I can do better than that." He clicked a key fob and his Jeep beeped from across the lot.

"How did your car get over here?"

"I phoned my bro and had it delivered from the bar."

"Nice." The mountains glowed from the last descending rays of the sun and the temperature had dropped. Soon it would be the longest day of the year. I loved this part of summer, and the mountains had a way of grounding me with a sense of calm. I felt freedom in the breeze, thankful I hadn't been arrested for something or other. "Can you drop me off at home?"

"Course." His head swiveled in all directions before he climbed into his Jeep.

I, too, glanced over my shoulder as we left the parking lot. I was relieved to have the sheriff's station in the rear view mirror. I felt a pang of conscience, but I was glad Lance had waited for me. I needed a ride and Ephraim hadn't provided one.

I dragged myself up the stairs and through the door

to my apartment. Axle ran in from the other room, his Rottweiler at his heels. "Where were you? I thought you'd be home a long time ago." He ran his hands over his hair, ruffling it.

"You were worried about me." I mock-punched his arm.

"No way." He denied it, but I could tell he was concerned. I toed off my shoes and barefooted it to the couch, and he followed me to the living room. "Spill. Where you been, Delaney?"

"I went with Lance to that cowboy bar on the outside of town and there was a drug raid. Ephraim was there." I sank into the couch cushions, lifted my feet, and hugged my knees to myself.

His eyes narrowed. "What?"

"You heard me. Keep up, here."

"Well, well, little miss perfect."

"Yeah, let's keep it on the down-low." My gaze went to the door as if I expected Kristen to knock. I was ashamed to tell her and hoped she wouldn't find out. "Anyway, you're the one who invited him in to play video games."

"But you're the one who followed him into the danger zone." He shook a finger at me.

The little twerp wasn't wrong. What was I doing? I walked right into a drug raid in the company of a drug dealer. This was no joke. Kris was right when she told me to be careful about who I hung out with. I hated to admit that Ephraim was right, too. Even though Lance was innocent of wrongdoing tonight—or he didn't get caught doing anything wrong tonight—was he a person I wanted to associate with?

I made my way to the kitchen and squeaked open the

refrigerator door. Boss leaned into the cold air and licked his chops. I expected to stare at empty shelves, but the fridge was crammed with groceries. Every shelf stuffed to overflowing. "Axle, did you go shopping?"

"Nah, your mom dropped by while you were gone."

I whirled toward him. "What?"

"She brought chicken broccoli." He indicated a covered casserole dish on the bottom shelf. "I'm hoping she shows up tomorrow, too. She said she was going to bake another cake."

Slamming the door shut, I said, "This is too much. No. No, no, no." Lord, no. Suddenly exhausted, I headed to bed, Boss leading the way. "I'm all in. See you in the morning."

****

We both slept late because it was Saturday and Axle didn't have to go to work. He and his dog came out from his room at ten and found me on the couch in my sleep shirt, staring like a zombie with a coffee in my hand and a loose, messy bun on top of my head—even though I was not going for the rock star look. I patted the cushion and Boss leapt up beside me while Axle went to the pot and poured a dark stream of coffee into a mug for himself. Then he nabbed a muffin from the box Mom left on the counter and wolfed it down in two swallows.

Once he flopped onto the couch across from me, he said, "Since you're hell bent on getting into trouble, I'm going to help you."

"Help me get into trouble?"

"Harty-har. That's a good one." He studied his phone screen. "You know what?"

I took the bait. "What?"

He handed his cell to me, so I palmed it and stared

at the screen. "A movie website? How's that help?" I handed it back.

He swiveled the screen around to show me. "Rory's aunt is Courtnee Clyborne, right?" I nodded. "These are a list of movies Courtnee Clyborne was in."

I blinked my sleepy eyes several times, hoping for the caffeine to kick in, and snatched the phone back. I ran through the titles. "I've watched some of these, but I don't remember seeing her in any of them."

"She had small parts."

"Okay, thanks." I shoved the phone back at him. "Thinking, thinking…I still don't understand how this helps. It doesn't seem to be important."

He swiped his screen and tossed me his phone again, open to Courtnee Clyborne's account, right at some interesting posts:

I don't enjoy getting stepped on. I watched Rick Rearden take my career away from me.

And…

That #sleezeball Rick Rearden promised me starring roles. He never came through.

"Gosh, she's complaining on social media about her own husband," I stated the obvious.

"Under her screen name, though."

"I stand corrected, Axle. This is important. It's a motive."

"Motive for what?" He urged me with a *go-on* look, peering out from under his lashes.

So, I told my roomie about the kidnapping. *I know, I know*, I promised Rory I wouldn't. But did Rory really expect me to hold to that? Double crap, he probably did. But I made Axle give me his word he wouldn't tell anyone. Of course, I'd just broken that same promise.

For once Axle didn't make any jokes. There's nothing funny about kidnapping. We talked more about the crime, and I was happy to have Axle to share it with.

After I showered and dressed, I took Boss for a walk and scooped kibble into his bowl, then dropped Axle at L&B Garage to work on his front-wheel drive Altima, once more out of commission. Pulling out of the lot, I signaled to turn onto Main Street where I brought my truck to an idle at the corner of Main and Columbine Court. I caught sight of a flashing light bar on a big wrecker ahead of me in the next block. Tanner. His tow truck left-turned onto Industrial Lane and I gunned my engine to keep up. He pulled into an empty parking lot and I cruised up beside him. I shoved out of my seat to meet him outside his cab.

After waiting a moment for the sounds of my truck's engine's knocking to cease, I said, "You've been busy, Tanner?"

"Yeah. I moved some cars up from Denver with my vehicle transporter the other day."

"Nice." I didn't have a transporter. My lightweight self-loader can haul up to seventy-five hundred pounds. That's just about every sedan, SUV, and light pickup, but I couldn't tow commercial vehicles, semis, work trucks, school buses, RVs, and I certainly couldn't move more than one vehicle at a time. "Heard from Savanah lately?"

He gave me a devilish smile. "She's still pressing me to move to Hollywood with her. She's got a sure thing coming up, a part in some movie. Just think, California, surf and sand." His blue eyes sparkled like sun on the ocean waves.

I struggled to keep the smile on my face. "But you're not going? You've got Tate and Annie to consider, remember?"

He gave a tired little sigh. "That's right. My brother and sister need me. And I guess I need them, too."

I nodded in understanding. And relief. "While we're on the topic, have you ever heard of the actress, Courtnee Clyborne?"

He tented his fingers as he thought for a moment, then he let out a low whistle. "I know who she is. She's in some B-movies. She's a babe. Why?"

"She's Rory's aunt."

"That I didn't know."

"Me, either. Well, you'd tell me if you changed your mind about California, right?"

"Not going to change my mind." Tanner maneuvered himself into his truck.

"Okay, see ya' later." I retreated to mine and gave him a wave before we parted ways. Tanner and I may not be romantically involved anymore, but I would miss him terribly if he left town. The idea clutched at my heart and I couldn't bear thinking about it.

Instead I considered that movie-nut Savanah. Since both Courtney and Savanah are actors and Rick Rearden's a movie producer, Savanah and the Reardens might be more than acquaintances, but how much more? Savanah had told me she'd met Rick, but implied they weren't chummy. She also knew who Rick's wife is, Courtnee Clyborne. What if the three of them were closer than she let on? Not just bumping into each other at a party? However, plenty of celebs lived in this town. That didn't mean Savanah spent time with the Reardens or they with her.

Still, Savanah was someone to question the next chance I got.

But right now, I had to take the opportunity to make money, so I performed a three-point turnaround to go the other direction and search for stalled cars. I could contemplate my next steps as I worked.

Mountain bikers, hikers, and campers swarmed Spruce Ridge in the summer, passing through my town and filling the coffee shops, restaurants, and stores selling outdoor gear. Only twelve thousand lived here year round, but in the warm months millions could pass by on the highway, and thousands made Spruce Ridge a stopping point. Rocky Mountain National Park had over four million visitors a year, and the park wasn't far away. The majesty of the mountains right outside my front door never failed to give me a thrill.

While on one of the frontage roads, I came across a pregnant woman by the side of her car, so I brought my truck to a stop and rolled down the window. "Looks like you need roadside assistance?"

"I was about to call my boyfriend." She tucked her phone into her purse. "This flat just happened."

I swung my high-heeled feet out of the cab. "I can change that for you."

She followed me to the back of her Wrangler Jeep, four-wheel drive. "Can you show me how to do it myself for next time? If there ever is a next time."

"Sure. Every woman should know how to change a tire. But I'm going to change it for you today."

At the beginning, my customers probably thought I was clueless with no towing skills whatsoever, and you know what? They might've been right. I'd only recently added this to my list of things I know how to do, and I was *sooo* glad I did since this was my second tire change in a week. I once helped three people who locked their keys in their cars in a single day. Now I haven't helped anyone with that problem in several months. It's what I like, every day being different. Yet, I'm anchored by the familiar workings of the truck and the steady rhythm of the life I've fallen into.

"If you can change a tire in those high heels, I can do it while pregnant." She rubbed her belly like expectant women do.

"I'm down with that." I struck a pose in my brown, wooden-soled clogs, a down-to-earth color. "But you're only going to watch this time." I escorted her to the back of the Jeep. The spare came off the mount once I'd removed the bolts with my cordless drill. "It's easier if you have the right tools. Not many people keep these drill attachments in their trunk. My jack is hydraulic, too."

She watched my every move while I demonstrated how to pull the lug nuts and position the jack. Then she insisted on paying and gave me a generous tip.

"You don't owe me that much."

"I insist."

I know my face turned red with pleasure and hoped my flush would be mistaken for a sunburn. A sense of accomplishment washed over me. I seemed to be handling the work much better than I used to. If you can believe this…I started out a failure—jackknifing cars on the tow bar and getting strange looks because of my footwear—and now I'm a successful business owner. And it's fun to be a girly tow truck operator. Yay, me.

I struck out for the coffee shop to reward myself with one of Kristen's heavenly brews, but gave up a sigh when I spied Mom's Chevrolet Suburban, rear-wheel drive, in the parking lot and Mom, herself, climbing the stairs to my apartment.

"It's good that I ran into you, Laney." She was grappling with a full laundry basket.

"Give me that." I snatched the heavy load from her hands to rest it on my hip. "My keys are in the front pocket of my purse."

She reached inside to take them and opened the door.

"You're here to do your laundry?" I asked as we crossed the kitchen. I set the basket on the table.

"No, these are your clothes, dear. I did your laundry."

I stared at the neatly folded clothes and recognized Axle's tee shirt on top with the slogan, *I love it when you fart*. "You didn't have to do that, Mom."

Her face fell. "I wanted to, hon."

I was quick to give her a hug. "Well, thanks, I appreciate it."

She reversed steps toward the door. "I'm off. My new bedroom suite and couch are going to be delivered today. See you soon."

"I'll walk down with you."

We stopped in the parking lot for another hug and I waited while she maneuvered her car onto Pine Street. I took a deep breath and with head down marched through the door into the coffee shop.

"Kris, what am I going to do about Mom?" I whined when I found my friend in her office.

"What's she done this time?"

I filled Kristen in, and the corners of her mouth twitched in laughter. "Not funny, Kris," I chided her. "I'm about to fling a bearing."

"Okay, but only you would complain about free

food and laundry service." She quickly sobered. "I'll pray about your situation and you should do the same."

I put the back of my hand to my forehead. "All right. Because I do need divine intervention."

Understatement!

Chapter 11

My phone chimed and Courtney's number lit up my screen. "You need another ride?" I asked.

"No. I thought you'd want to know the sheriff returned my money."

"Omigod! I can't believe it!" I slapped my cheek with my palm. After I'd last met with Ephraim, I didn't think the money was close to being released.

"Why don't you come over? We have some things to discuss. Be discreet."

"Sure," I said to an empty line since she'd hung up.

I exchanged my truck for my Fiat and took my Fiat to Rory's. I got out and made my way around the Rearden's main house to the red-brick cottage. Courtney pushed open the white door and yanked me inside. She stuck her head back out, craned her neck all around, then slammed the door shut behind us. The room was dark with heavy furniture, a black desk, and a hard-looking sofa. Rory sat on the sofa with one foot propped on his knee.

"So, you got the money back," I said.

"We picked up the cash." Rory gulped and slitted a glance at his aunt. "The money's been returned."

"I'm shocked," I admitted.

His aunt said, "The sheriff told me there's not enough evidence to prove a crime was committed. They can't link the money to the hand."

"No evidence of a crime," Rory repeated.

"Huh. Ephraim never called to let me know." In fact, he'd given me the certain impression the money wasn't going to be released anytime soon.

Courtney lowered herself into the chair behind the desk and rested her elbows on the surface. "The sheriff told me the hand is being treated as a separate investigation, and it remains ongoing because no one showed up anywhere with that kind of an injury."

"Okay." I rubbed the back of my neck. "Well, at least you got the money. Did you deposit it in a bank?" Half a million in cash? I'd be nervous handling that amount, but then I'd never had that amount. Or anywhere close to that amount.

"No. The kidnapper called when we got home. Whoever it is must've been watching us. The person probably saw us leaving the sheriff's station with the duffel bags."

I raised my eyebrows. "I'm amazed they didn't just grab the bags."

"In the middle of the sheriff's parking lot?" she snickered.

"Oh yeah, I guess they wouldn't. So, what did the kidnapper say?" I sank onto the hard sofa next to Rory and leaned forward.

"Another drop is scheduled, this time at the Park-N-Ride. I admit, I'm scared. The kidnapper said this was my last chance and nothing can go wrong this time. They used a voice distortion device again."

"I'm going with Auntie," Rory said.

I said, "I want to come, too, but will it be safe? Maybe we need protection." Like a couple of carloads of sheriff deputies.

"Where are we going to get protection? No police." Courtney's voice sounded stern.

I went over other options in my mind. There weren't any. Except one. "I have a friend who'd know how to handle everything. We could get my friend involved."

"Not the police," Courtney said again for the *nth* time.

"Farthest thing from it." I shook my head. "Does anyone else know about the drop-off other than the three of us?

Courtney shook her head and Rory said, "No, no one but us. Just us here in this room."

I launched into Lance Palmero's theory that a new drug kingpin was in town trying to take over the territory. And Iceman's MO was hacking off hands.

"No freakin' way," Rory said.

"Way." I fixed him with a serious look. "This is very dangerous. If it is Iceman, don't you want some protection to come along with us?" I warmed to my idea.

Courtney tapped her nose as if considering it, then asked, "Can you call your friend? We have to make the drop in an hour."

"I'll call him now." I got busy on my phone and explained the situation—Lance wasn't fazed by the news—then told the other two, "He's on the way."

Rory brought up, "Should we put the foot in with the bags of money?"

"No!" I might have shrieked that. "You have to give that foot to the police."

Courtney conceded, "All right, all right. We'll give it to the police, but not until I get my husband back." A knock on the door brought her out of her chair and she rushed to answer it, performing the same eye-sweeping survey of the surroundings before letting Lance inside.

I introduced him. "This is Lance, but he goes by Demented." I saved that part until now. Rory and his aunt looked alarmed, which is why I didn't mention it before. Although the lightning bolt tattoo across his forehead and the barbell body piercing could've contributed to the fear in their eyes.

After we showed him the foot, Lance said, "You done right not giving it to the police. How'd you cut the cops out, anyway?"

Courtney said, "I arranged for the people in Hollywood to lie about Rick being on the set so I could keep the police from intervening. This is why they don't know about the kidnapping."

"Good move." Lance rose. "Let's book." We all checked our phones for the time, except for Courtney who looked at her mother-of-pearl watch.

Courtney said, "You two will need to drive separately. I don't want to scare the kidnapper with a car full of passengers."

Lance's eyes locked on me. "Del, why don't we ride together?"

"Okay, but I'm driving."

The four of us fell in line walking the distance to the front of the mansion, but stopped in mid-stride when we got to the driveway. The neighbor from across the street, James Atkins, was talking to Rory's dad, Randy, on the front steps.

"Courtney, I'm glad to run into you." Randy gave her a lopsided grin so like his son's and brother's.

"Yes?" Courtney glanced down at her fancy watch.

"Have you heard from Rick?" Randy's smile wavered as he took in the tall gangster standing behind me.

Courtney yanked up her head with the wide-eyed look of a hiker caught at altitude in a March blizzard. "Not today."

James made a gagging sound, then coughed into his hand. Courtney's head jerked toward him, and they exchanged look for look.

She broke the connection and her gaze went back to Randy. "Do you need Rick for something? I might see him this afternoon." Her leather boot tapped with impatience. I wasn't sure we'd get Rick back that soon, but Courtney seemed to think so.

Rory didn't speak, so I remained quiet, too. An unlit cigarette jutted out of Lance's mouth, but he boosted a smile in my direction.

Randy shoved his hands in to his pockets. "If you do see him, tell him to call me." He turned toward James and said, "I'll catch you later, then?" and James nodded. Randy went inside the house, and James glanced again at Courtney.

"What are you looking at?" she asked him.

James pinched the bridge of his bulbous nose. "Nothing." He whirled on his heel and vanished down the long driveway. Courtney breathed like she was hyperventilating and quickened her pace toward her husband's Volvo. She practically threw herself into the front seat. Her nerves were making me jittery, too.

I reached her car in a few quick steps. "We'll be right behind you."

She nodded at me through her open window and took deep breaths in and out. Rory buckled himself into the passenger side and she put the Volvo in gear.

Lance and I bounded over to the Fiat. We followed

Courtney and Rory out of the neighborhood at a normal speed. Once on the main road, she floored it toward the highway in the direction of the bus stop, and I followed on her bumper. I could imagine how she felt, since my heart rate skipped, too, like I was supercharged on caffeine. I tried to calm my racing thoughts, keeping in mind Lance was here with me. I was safe. What could go wrong?

Famous last words.

Courtney parked the Volvo behind a row of buses as instructed, and I slid my pint-sized Fiat in between two SUVs, almost completely hiding my car from sight, but not blocking our view of Courtney's Volvo. My palms were sweating so I ran them down my jeans.

"Lance, how do you think this is going to go down?" I needed some reassurance.

"We need to see to it those two don't act stupid." His eyes scoped out the parking lot with people queuing up for the next bus.

"Act stupid? What do you mean?"

"Iceman could snatch those two along with the wad." The gangster gazed straight ahead, immobile, looking calm, while I stifled the scream at the back of my throat, ready to explode from the tension.

"So, you think Iceman's the kidnapper?"

"Don't you?"

A Chevrolet Suburban, rear-wheel drive, stopped in front of us, obstructing our field of vision. An attractive blonde my mom's age got out and strode in our direction. Wait, it was Mom.

Mom?
My mom?
Good. God.

I shot out of my Fiat and ran towards her. As I approached, she grabbed both of my arms. "Laney, I'm so glad I spotted you. I have a real crisis on my hands. I need—"

"—Not now, Mom. Now's not a good time."

"When I saw your car, I just had to tell you—"

"—Mom, not now. Wait, how'd you notice my car?"

"I'd recognize your tiny silver Fiat anywhere." She gave me an up and down look. "You all right?"

"No." When I saw her blanch, I changed it to, "Yes, I'm fine. Mom you need to leave." I glanced over at the gangster in my Fiat. He was flailing his arms around, then stopped and patted his jacket, mouthing, "You need help?"

There was no doubt about it, I totally needed help. But not his kind of help. There was a knife, or even a gun, in his jacket. He was packing.

I held up my hand, palm out to indicate, *no*, then I led Mom back to her driver's door. "Meet me at my apartment. I'll get there as soon as I can." When she started to protest, I said, "Mom, you need to leave. Now."

Understanding filled her eyes. "You're on a job?"

"Yes." Close enough to the truth. She thought I was on a repo, which could be dangerous, but not as dangerous as this.

She got in her car. "Okay, hon. Don't be long." She gave me a bright smile as she pulled away.

I glanced back at Lance and saw his eyes open wide before narrowing down to a straight line. Then I swung my gaze over my shoulder. The Volvo was gone.

Poofed. Not there. Disappeared.

I sprang back to my Fiat and dove inside. "Where'd

they go?"

"They're ghost. Who was that crazy lady?" Lance wanted to know.

"My mother. I didn't know she was going to show up here."

"I getcha. I got one of them, and a baby momma, too."

I didn't have time to visualize Lance as a dad. "Call Rory. Find out where they went." I handed him my phone with Rory's number on the screen, then I pressed the accelerator down to the floor and the Fiat lurched forward.

Rory must've had the phone in his hand because Lance talked into my cell right away. Lance disconnected and patted the top of my head. "It's okay. They're straight. They're headed back to the crib."

"Where's that?"

"They called it the guesthouse. I assumed they meant the crib. They handed off the bank to the snatcher."

"Is Rick with them?"

He made a small side-to-side motion with his head. "No. The 'napper didn't give up the man."

I hit my head against the seatback a couple of times. There was a heavy silence between us the rest of the short drive.

As soon as we pushed through the door to the guesthouse, I asked Courtney, "What happened? We lost sight of you."

Courtney paced in front of the sofa, and Rory stood at the window, kneading his forehead with his knuckles. Courtney held out a clown mask with a bald dome, orange scruff around the ears, and an orange bozo nose, but all I could do is stare at her. I expected tears and hysteria, but what I received was a steely-eyed look.

She said, "The person was wearing one of these masks. I handed the duffel bags out the window, he transferred them into a gray minivan, no license plates, and when I asked about Rick, he didn't speak. He only handed me this mask, just like the one he was wearing."

"What does it mean?" I asked.

"He still has Uncle Rick." Rory had on an anguished expression. I tried to maintain my composure but tears gathered in the back of my throat and sympathy gutted my stomach.

Lance said, "Iceman wouldn't wear no mask."

Courtney asked him, "You don't think the kidnapper is Iceman?"

"The mask's not his MO."

I asked Courtney, "Can you tell us anything about the guy's appearance? Just one person, right?"

"Right. That mask was distracting and I didn't see his face, of course."

"Are you sure it was a man?"

"No. It could've been a woman, I guess."

"Did you get a sense of the person's height?"

"Average for a man. Maybe 5'11" and slim."

"What about the hands? Small? Manicured nails? Long nails?"

"The person wore bulky gloves. And had on baggy clothes, too. He didn't speak at all, just took the money, handed me the mask."

"That is all so vague. Average, thin. Maybe a man. Maybe a woman. Should we turn the mask in to the police?" When everyone shook their heads, I said, "Put it in a plastic bag. There might be fingerprints on it. If

Rick doesn't show up soon, I don't care what you say, I'm calling the cops and turning in the mask. And the foot."

Courtney said, "The kidnapper will call me again, I'm sure. He got the money, I'll get Rick back, and I just have to believe he'll call and tell me where Rick is."

I turned to Lance for reassurance that this was true, but we only gaped at each other. What happened to Rick Rearden wasn't something I was willing to dwell on. "Rory, contact me as soon as you hear anything. I have something else I need to take care of now, but call me no matter what time it is."

He vaguely nodded, so Lance and I stepped outside. "Lance?" My legs were wobbly. I stumbled into him and buried my face against his chest.

He held me steady. "I'll catch the word on the street," he said in the cryptic way I was starting to understand. "You go talk to your momma."

"Thanks for everything, Lance."

"Of course, Del." He touched his gang tattoo. "I owe you, remember?"

We got into our respective cars. I don't recall the drive home, and simply found myself climbing the stairs to my apartment. When I walked inside, Mom was there, stirring a pot on the stove with an apron around her waist.

I plopped my purse on the counter, and Boss came over wagging his tail, but after I gave him a head-scrunch he shot back to his spot at Mom's feet. The scent of sauteed beef and onion touched my nose and a peaceful feeling came over me. Mom, dog, food.

"What are you making?"

"Cheeseburger casserole. I'm just browning the meat now. I know how you love my casseroles."

"What's this about a crisis? You mentioned a crisis at the Park-N-Ride?"

She swiveled toward me and waved a wooden spoon around. Boss followed the motion with his eyes, hoping drops would fall to the floor.

"It's bad, Laney, real bad."

"What? Tell me."

"My condo's been infested by bugs. Little gnats everywhere. I have to put a coaster on top of my wine glass or the nasty things get in and become floaters."

This *was* a major crisis.

"I bought one of those safari nets to sleep under, but that doesn't help me at the stove." She turned back to the sizzling pan. "I can't even cook there."

I *had* prayed that God would send her home to Will like Kristen told me to. Had God sent her a plague to drive her out of the condo? Kristen always said God answered prayers in ways we didn't expect. Was this all my fault?

"How'd you get inside my apartment?" I asked.

"Kris gave me an extra key."

And I thought she was my best friend. I managed to ask, all casual-like, "Did you call an exterminator?"

"Yes." She consulted the clock on the microwave. "They should be at the condo now, but I can't stay there tonight. I can camp here with you, can't I? I brought my overnight bag."

I choked out, "Of course. I need to use the bathroom. I'll be right back." I scooted down the hall to my room, stuffed a pillow over my mouth, and screamed into it. Then I dialed my stepdad. "Hey, Will. What's this about you and Mom having a disagreement?"

"Is your mom in Spruce Ridge with you?"

"Yes, she's here right now. You didn't know?"

"She told me she'd purchased a condo. She didn't say where."

"Her condo is ten minutes from my apartment." The other end of the line went as quiet as a Tesla's engine. "Will?"

"Yeah?"

"You need to talk to Mom, tell her you want her back. You do want her back, right?" I could sense his hesitation over the phone. "Will!"

"She stepped over the line, Delaney. But, you're right, we need to talk. I'll call her."

I breathed a huge sigh of relief as I disconnected. But when I walked back into the kitchen and her phone rang, Mom didn't pick up.

We ate the cheeseburger casserole at the kitchen table, then I made up a bed on the couch. For me. I gave Mom my bedroom. At least I got a yummy meal out of the evening, and Axle would inhale the leftovers when he got home.

****

My phone buzzed in the middle of the night. I trod softly into the kitchen to answer it and spoke quietly into the phone. After tapping on Axle's door and whispering for him to come with me, I realized I couldn't show up in my pjs and robe, so I cracked open the door to my bedroom, hoping to sneak in for some clothes.

Before I'd tiptoed halfway to my closet, Mom sat up. "What's the matter, Laney? Everything okay?"

"Oh, sorry. I have a tow. Just let me grab some jeans."

She swung her legs out from under the blanket. "Can I come, too? I'll only lay here and worry until you get back home."

I blinked and ran a hand across my bleary eyes. "Sure." She caught me at a weak moment.

"What'll I wear?" She followed me to the closet. "I didn't pack a change of clothes in my overnight bag except for my linen dress pants, and they're white. Can I borrow something of yours?"

I handed her a clean pair of jeans and a hoodie, and scrounged into the jeans I'd worn earlier today. She took hers to the bathroom and came out looking like a slightly older, blonde version of me, even right down to the heels.

She said, "I'd ask for a pair of tennis shoes, but you know I wear two sizes smaller than you do. Put your heels on, too. Don't we both have to wear them?"

"I might as well." Instead of the sensible boots I normally wore for night tows, I returned to the closet for my black stilettos. Black for resigned.

Note to self: Call Will again asap.

When we both strode into the kitchen, Axle did a double-take. "You guys could be twins, except for your red hair, Delaney."

"Funny." I slapped the top of his bedhead, while Mom beamed and ran a hand down the backside of her slim jeans. The two of them followed me out to the car. Axle stuffed himself into the tiny rear seat of the Fiat, and we drove in silence to get my truck, because Axle dozed, and I was struck speechless. The caller was a doctor from the city hospital, so I figured Mom would be safe. If the call had been from Axle's old trailer park, forget it. I wouldn't have let her ride along. Even I wouldn't have wanted to go there.

I drove my truck down the ramp into the underground parking lot at the Spruce Ridge Hospital and spotted a man in scrubs who looked like he was about fifteen. His Lexus, rear-wheel drive, blocked the exit ramp on the B Level.

"It just stalled on me, and I can't leave it here," he explained.

"I see that."

"I'm Dr. Jacquin, by the way."

"I'm Delaney Morran, this is Axle, and this is, uh, Eve." I gestured vaguely at Mom.

I pulled Axle aside. "Take Mom and stand over by that pillar." I indicated a safe space several yards away.

He mumbled, his eyes in slits, "Okay," and I could tell he was still in that half asleep-half awake state and planned to stay that way.

"Please stand to the side, too," I asked the doctor and he went to join Ax and Mom. I maneuvered my big truck around to position the crossbar at the rear of the Lexus and hit the button to lower the boom and extend the claws. I popped the truck's gear into drive and was about to hit the gas when the Lexus dropped to the ground with a loud bang that echoed through the concrete structure. Mom screamed, and Axle and Dr. Jacquin jumped like they were having spasms.

I looked in my rearview mirror to see the Lexus had fallen off the boom. We all watched as the vehicle began to roll slowly away and came coasting to a stop nose-in to the far wall.

I tucked my head down and exited the cab. Dr. Jacquin rushed up to me. "I thought you were going to tow my car out of here, but this is perfect. I'll just have my mechanic come by and take a look at it tomorrow."

"What?" I wasn't sure I heard him right.

"You did a very nice job getting my car back into

my parking space."

Sure enough, painted on the wall above the Lexus was Dr. Jacquin's name.

"How much do I owe you?" he asked.

"Ah, nothing. Since I didn't have to tow your car anywhere, let's just forget it." I'd like to forget it, anyway.

"Are you sure? That was an amazing stunt."

"It was, wasn't it?" I agreed.

My mom said, "I had no idea this is what you did, Laney," as she climbed inside the truck. Axle got in the backseat with the doctor and smirked at me through his reflection in the mirror.

Mom and Dr. Jacquin chatted over the back of the seat like old friends and she told him how I'm the high-heeled tow truck driver as if she was actually proud of me for a change. After I dropped the doctor off at his house and Axle climbed in front with me, he chuckled and said, "You're whacko, Delaney."

I pointed a raised eyebrow at him. "You don't think I conquered that move?"

He made a derisive noise. "A negative on the no-way scale."

"Well…"

Mom said, "What's this?"

Axle came to my rescue. "That was totally smooth, real slick, Delaney." He looked back at my mom. "Your daughter really knows how to keep a grip. How to keep things under control. Yeah, she had that move locked down." He laughed at his own joke because I hadn't locked down the tires with straps.

I gave him a look that said *don't overdo.*

****

The next morning I wanted some time to myself, so I threw my jeans and sweatshirt back on and headed down the stairs. I didn't even stick around my apartment for coffee, I just had to get out of there. When I almost reached my car, a man came around the back fender and stopped me in my tracks. The man had dark eyes and hair and was an inch or so short of six feet tall, nice-looking except for a couple of missing front teeth. Flanking him were two taller men with muscles. Big muscles. Muscles on muscles.

Iceman and a couple of heavies.

I recognized the gangster from the photo Parker Smith, the drug task force guy, had showed me. The two with him were likely his enforcers. The ones who cut off body parts? *Gulp!*

"Are you Del?" Iceman asked.

"What do you want?" My gaze flew to the upstairs window. Mom and Axle were both still asleep in the apartment. Was Iceman going to force himself in? Was my family safe? I felt a surge of panic and took a deep centering breath.

"This is about the booty in the backseat. I want the money. It's mine and I want it."

"I don't have it. Courtney gave it to the clown. Wasn't that you?" My lips trembled as I spoke.

"I ain't no clown. But, speaking of booty, you have a nice booty. I'd like to get my hands on that booty." He reached over and pinched my butt.

Dread raced around my veins, and I swatted his hand away. "Stop that. Who calls a girl's ass a booty anymore? That's not politically correct."

One of the muscles said, "Yeah, Iceman, she's right. It's not a booty, she's got nice tail. You want to get your hands on her tail."

The other one said, "No, tail's not good, either."

"How about buns?"

"No."

"Tush?"

"Not respectful."

I nodded. "I agree. That's offensive." But who knew gangsters would care about being PC.

"Shuddup, you dumbasses." A powerful rage lit Iceman's eyes. He looked straight at me. "This is my territory now. You get me that money, you hear? And it better all be there. The talk around town is that you helped yourself to some bills."

"I didn't. And I don't know where the money is now. If you're the boss around here, then you know where to find it."

I put on a lot of bravado as I fumbled open my Fiat, cranked the key, and swerved out of the lot. I parked behind a blue spruce down the street and watched as Iceman climbed into a gold, late-model Chevrolet Corvette, rear-wheel drive, and the other two got in a second car. Once the vehicle exited the lot and disappeared down Pine, I waited to make sure they didn't come back. After ten minutes, I took off in the other direction.

I hit Main Street and accelerated. When I got to the highway, I went from thirty to sixty in a matter of seconds, the Fiat wailing as I raced along.

My car found its way to the side of I-70 at mile marker 421. I trudged down the verge, slipping on pine needles, through the trees to an outcropping of rock. From there the mountain vista offered a hundred-mile view of pointed peaks spearing the sky, sharply in focus in the thin, clear air. A dangerous, deadly spot. Even standing twenty feet from the edge gave me a dizzy sensation, so I turned around and hiked back to the white cross that stuck up from the ground.

A typically strong wind blew, whipping strands of hair across my face and causing me to wrap my arms around myself. Tears pressed at my eyes, and my gut hurt like there was motor oil in my stomach. Not for the first time did I wish Dad were here with me. But he wasn't here. He was never here for me, having been absent all of my childhood. I'd always intended to contact him, but before I'd done so, he'd been forced off the road at this spot where I'd erected the white cross. I had so many questions, including why he didn't keep in touch with me…why he left me his tow truck…and who caused his fatal accident. Everything was so baffling. How could I help anyone else when I couldn't sort through my own confusion?

To escape out of the endless wind, I got back inside my Fiat and turned my phone over and over in my hand.

Even though Iceman's name was at the top of my suspect list, someone else had interfered at the drop-off. That much was obvious. Perhaps the person in the clown mask intercepted the drop and snatched the money out from under Iceman's nose. And now he was trying to find the cash and thought I knew where it was. *Moi?* Like I would know. He had more resources than I did—goon one and goon two. But how could the gangster have let the money slip through his fingers? A brutal and powerful man like him would not have let anything happen to his money. Iceman was a movie villain on steroids.

I had to consider the possibility that the gang boss

was not working alone. If he had an accomplice, that person could've helped abduct Rick from the party, then double-crossed Iceman and taken the ransom money, no matter how inconceivable that was.

If there was a double-cross, what was going to happen to Rick? It was downright weird how Courtney was going about this whole ransom payoff. When I'd left her, she seemed detached, like she was hopeful, almost confident, that the kidnapper would call with Rick's location and he would be released. How could she be so certain? Is that why she wasn't working with the police?

As for me, I'm not so hopeful and I'm not so detached, either. I can't be. I can't say this is someone else's problem and walk away. For Rory's sake (as well as my own) I needed to find Uncle Rick. And the money, too. And since someone other than Iceman had the money, that was the place to start. I had to consider everyone, either as a suspect or an accomplice.

I put down my phone and found the list of guests in my purse. Of the names, these were the only ones I recognized:

Parker Smith. With the Drug Force, so an unlikely kidnapper. But he was at James' party and that in itself is suspicious.

Savanah Rivers. Even a less likely suspect, this flighty California girl.

Lance Palmero. My honorary brother in the Thunder Knuckles gang. It can't be him. He was with me at the drop-off, plus he would not work with a rival gang member like Iceman.

I didn't know anybody else on the list

What about James Atkins? I knew nothing about him, other than he liked to host parties.

Courtney Rearden. Don't forget her. She had motive, means, and opportunity. Rory's aunt was one of the last people to see his uncle before he vanished. They had an argument at the party. According to her posts, she was angry with her husband for not casting her in better movie roles. Or was there another woman? The one Rick went upstairs with? These were Hollywood types, you know. Or, how's this for an idea? Was Courtney Iceman's accomplice? Would a wannabe movie star like Courtney collaborate with a gang boss like Iceman? I didn't like her much, but she is Rory's aunt, so I wanted Iceman's partner-in-crime to be someone else.

The clown had to know about the drop-off time and place, and no one knew other than Courtney, Rory, Lance, me…and the kidnapper. Courtney was the only one of us with a motive…except money gave everyone a motive. Anyone willing to kidnap Rick Rearden for five hundred thousand dollars had a motive. Courtney was at the clown payoff, too, but that didn't eliminate her, or any of us, if one of us had a helper. *Arg!* See what I mean? Baffling. As tangled and twisted as a winding road up a mountain pass.

What about the severed hand and foot? What did the dismemberments have to do with the kidnapping, unless the body parts really did belong to Rick? Who would be strong enough to use a saw to hack through bones? The two goons, that's who. But to what purpose? It didn't make sense that anyone would go to those lengths.

I snatched my phone back up and placed a call to Rory. "I'm glad you phoned," Rory said when I reached him. "The kidnapper never called again. I'm so worried about Uncle Rick. What are they going to cut off next? An arm or a leg?"

"Those body parts may not be his, remember?" I tried to make my tone soothing, even though I'd just had the same suspicions. "Do you have time to talk? Can I swing by?"

"I have a few minutes if you get here quick. Come on over. I'll be here."

I flipped the Fiat around and took I-70 back to Spruce Ridge. Rory waited for me in the driveway when I came to a stop.

Savanah Rivers stood next to him with her hand on his arm. "All right, then. You'll call me, won't you?"

"Sure will. I'll call first thing. Right away, don't you worry." Rory's head bobbed up and down.

"Oh look. Here's Johnny." She flapped one hand at me in a wave, then hurried across the street with her head down.

I asked Rory. "You two going out now?"

"No, no. She was asking about Aunt Courtney. Savanah wants to talk to my aunt about some movie role or another. Movie business, you know." He opened the front door of his mansion and nodded me through. "She doesn't know what's going on."

"She was at the party, so she's a suspect, Rory." And an irritating person, trying to get Tanner to move with her to California. Of course Tanner won't go, he has his brother and sister to look after.

"Huh?" Rory halted in the entryway and I almost barreled into him from behind.

"Savanah was at the party with your uncle."

He pulled his hand down his face. "Oh, yeah, but a lot of people were there."

"Rory, Iceman was outside my apartment this morning. He's the drug dealer that Lance thought might be involved in the kidnapping."

He turned hopeful eyes on me. "Does he have Uncle Rick?"

"I don't know. I wish I did…" I stopped speaking and gave a little sigh. "So, no call from the kidnapper?"

"No call. No word at all. I need to go to a meeting that started five minutes ago. Sorry, Laney. But did Iceman say anything else? Anything?"

I had my hand on the door knob. "He didn't say much."

"No clue at all? Nothing about Uncle? Are you going to talk to him again? How did you leave it?"

"I'm hoping I don't run into that man again, but I'm still working on figuring this out. I'll let you get to your meeting, Rory." I left it at that and let the door fall shut behind me on the way out.

The encounter with the gang boss was creepy and scary and dangerous. I really should call Ephraim about Iceman, but I hesitated. I'd promised not to bring in the cops, and the confrontation with Iceman didn't change anything.

Plus, if I didn't talk about it, maybe it didn't really happen.

Chapter 12

Having second thoughts, I decided to text Ephraim. Not to bring up Iceman, but for reassurance that the sheriff was nearby if I needed him.

I wondered why Ephraim hadn't called me to let me know, but typed anyway:

—*Thanks for returning the $$ to Courtney.—*

I tossed my phone on the seat and started up the Fiat. The short stretch of road leading home was empty of traffic, so when my cell rang, I picked up.

"I got your text and thought I'd call to say you're welcome." He sounded like he was glad to hear from me.

"Uh, thanks."

"How are you doing? Staying out of trouble?" The image of Iceman and his muscled friends swam in my vison and I blanked out for a moment. "Delaney, are you there?"

"Yeah, I'm here."

"You're not with Lance Palmero, are you?"

"No. No, no, no."

"What's the matter?"

"Nothing."

He'd probably heard the uncertainty in my voice. "There's something you're not telling me." *No kidding!*

"I'm fine." I felt the blood rising in my cheeks. "So, Courtney said the investigation into the hand is still ongoing. Did you learn anything new?"

"No."

"No? Or you can't tell me?"

"No, nothing new."

"Hey, I just got home, so I'll let you go." I glided the Fiat into my usual spot and glanced around the apartment's parking lot. Iceman's gold Corvette was thankfully absent.

"Not so fast. You're holding back. Something's wrong, come on, you can tell me, what is it?" His deep, strong voice made my breath catch in the back of my throat.

There was so much I did want to talk to him about. Not only Iceman's threats, but the kidnapping, the chopped-off hand and foot, and everything else. I'd never kept this kind of information from Ephraim before. I said, "I promised to keep quiet about it."

"I'm on my way over."

"All right, Ephraim." I melted a little inside. Since it was Sunday and he was off work, I should've guessed he wouldn't be too busy to meet.

I ran up the steps and through the door, stopping long enough to give Boss a quick scrunch on the head and a promise of a walk later. I finger combed my long curls, then applied some concealer over my dark freckles and lip gloss over my pale lips. I didn't look too bad in my tee shirt and bib-overall shorts with chunky ankle boots.

When the bell ding-donged, I opened the door to Ephraim. Cowboy boots. Big belt buckle. Butt-hugging jeans. Yeah, that guy. Out of uniform Ephraim was even more eye-catching, and well, drool-worthy. I wanted to fan myself.

"Come on in."

He lowered his hat from his head and ducked through the entryway. I walked him back to the living room sofa and we took seats next to each other. Boss jumped on the other loveseat and settled his muzzle between his paws.

"I'm worried about you, *bella.*" He sat back as if waiting for my response.

"No news on the hand, you said?" I asked.

He sighed. "We're not releasing any new information at this time. And I'm here to find out what's up with you, not to talk about my investigation, but yours. Have you been questioning witnesses?"

"This isn't a good time for that quit-investigating speech, Ephraim."

He scooted closer, making me painfully aware of his proximity. "I won't give you that speech, but let me help you, Delaney. If you're in a tricky situation, I want to help. Besides, I always appreciate your insight. I wish you'd tell me what you know. I'm not sure why you won't this time."

"I just can't."

"But why?"

I chewed the inside of my cheek. "I'm still mad at you."

"What?" The creases deepened in his forehead.

Was it possible I was overreacting about the blonde at the mall? Did I need to let go of my hurt feelings? I blew out a sigh. Now wasn't the time to think about our relationship.

"I have come into some information, but I made a promise not to go to the police. When I can tell you, I will." I'd agreed to keep it quiet, and I'm not just another ditzy redhead in heels after all. I could keep a secret—

except from Axle, and now Lance too—as well as a promise. I placed my hand against his cheek. "I swear."

"I'm sorry for whatever I've done." He captured my fingers and placed his lips on my palm, then put a hand on the back of my neck to draw me in to a kiss…that knocked me breathless.

Yowzah!

Well, maybe I should tell him. What would it hurt?

"Ephraim…" I stopped speaking and listened to heels pounding up the outside staircase announcing someone coming to the door. The key turned in the lock and we jumped apart.

"Hello," Mom sang out. Boss ran over and leapt on her knees. "I'm excited to see you, too. Did you miss me? Did you miss me? Of course you did." She made kissy sounds at the Rottweiler. "I brought stuff to make brownies. You used to love brownies, Delaney. Oh, hello, Ephraim. I'll bet you like brownies, too." She started unpacking a cloth grocery bag onto the counter. Sugar, flour, bars of chocolate, milk, eggs, a bottle of vanilla.

"Hello, Eve." Ephraim stood, then extended a hand and pulled me up with him.

We spent a few minutes leaning against the counter while Mom organized the measuring cups and spoons and a mixing bowl.

"Bugs all gone?" I asked her.

"The exterminators told me to give it twenty-four hours." She said to Ephraim by way of explanation, "I bought a condo at the ski resort and it was infested with bugs." She made a *tssking* sound.

His eyebrows elevated in a question and I returned a shake of the head, indicating I'd tell him later.

Mom glanced at the stove clock. "Those twenty-four hours are almost up. I can head over after the brownies come out of the oven." She turned to me. "I won't need to stay here tonight, but thanks for letting me sleep over last night."

"Of course, Mom."

"I meant to ask you how that repo went at the bus stop? Did you get the car? Was that man you were with helping you?"

"No, I didn't get the car. Maybe next time." I flashed Mom a look to drop it.

"Who was helping you?" Ephraim asked. "Tanner?"

"No," Mom and I said at the same time.

"One of Axle's friends." I felt my cheeks grow warm and cursed my pale complexion.

Ephraim gave me a long, hard look. "Well, I'll get going, Delaney. You'll keep me in the loop, right?"

I did a brush-off flap of my hand. "Sure."

There was a quick narrowing of his eyes. "See you later."

After he clattered down the stairs, Mom said, "What was that about?"

"Oh, nothing. Let me find a baking dish." I snatched up my hair to turn it into a braid, then muddled through the cabinets until I found a pan, realizing I'd been saved from further entanglement with Ephraim by two blondes. Mom and the blonde at the mall. But I didn't feel like thanking either of them at the moment.

"Did you notice I cleaned your fridge?" Mom asked while pouring the batter into the pan.

"Yeah, and the bathroom, too. Mom, you shouldn't be cleaning up after me. And Axle."

"Well, don't tell anyone. It's still not up to my

standards."

"I wouldn't dream of it." That was one secret that wouldn't be hard to keep. And my bathroom tiles never gleamed like that before. Jeez.

Mom took off once the brownies were cooling on the stovetop, and Axle showed up just in time to snarf down a few.

He sprawled on the couch with the TV tuner. "Want to watch a movie?" he asked as he swiped the crumbs off his sweatshirt.

I plunked down next to him ready for some stress-free, down time. "How about one with Courtnee Clyborne?"

"I'll find one." He clicked the remote to search and discovered a thriller called *Dead or Not* with Courtnee's name buried in the credits as "screaming girl two." I microwaved popcorn and we both settled in with Boss between us. It was so bad we laughed through most of it. Axle said, "Let's see how many of her movies we can stand to watch."

We finished two more by midnight. The last one, *Dead or Not Revisited*, garnered some good reviews and appeared to have a cult following. Everyone's hands were chopped off except for the main star's. There were chopped-off hands in nearly every scene.

"This can't be a coincidence, can it?" I asked my lil' cuz'.

"I think it's been done a lot. I mean, I've seen it before." He got on his phone to make a query. "Yeah, there are a ton of thrillers with severed hands. It's the bomb."

"What about severed feet?"

"*Texas Chain Shaw Massacre.*"

"This points to Courtney. Is the wife part of the kidnapping scheme?"

"Sorry, what?" Axle had been absorbed with his screen. He set his phone down and threw Boss a piece of popcorn. The slobbery monster caught and swallowed it at the same time.

"Say Courtney wanted to get rid of her husband? She hacks off a hand. Then a foot. She's going to get rid of him piece by piece. It's suspicious that she won't call the police."

"You've been watching too many of these stupid flicks." Axle shook his head.

"Well, I don't trust her. It's all very, very suspicious."

"It doesn't take a genius to figure that out." He flipped my braid and it flew up and hit me in the face.

"Hey. Stop that." I smoothed my plait back in place. "Look at the time."

"Yeah, I'm done." Axle stifled a yawn. We said goodnight and each went to our rooms.

I thought I'd have nightmares from all the horror movies, but I slept soundly until my phone rang. I opened one eye to look at the clock on the bedside table. Two in the a.m. I groaned. It can't be. I opened the other eye and found the clock still blinking *two, two, two.*

After taking the call, I woke Axle to come with me. No way was I going out there alone and risk running into a serial killer who dismembers victims with a sharp-bladed tool. I guess those horror movies were affecting me after all. We locked the apartment up behind us, picked up my tow truck, and peeled off for the highway. My truck sailed up the traffic-free mountain pass and breezed down the other side, until we came up to an older

Toyota Sequoia, rear-wheel drive.

The stalled vehicle disgorged a thin, anemic-looking man, so I shimmied out of the truck to greet him. "Hello. You called for a tow?"

"That was me. Thanks for coming out." The thin man glanced at my logo. "You're the one who found that buttload of cash?"

"Yeah." I didn't bother to deny it and told him my charges for transport into town. I processed his credit card while Axle operated the boom to raise the back end of the Sequoia and secured the wheels with tie-downs.

"So, finders-keepers, right?" The man grinned and rubbed his hands.

"Wrong. The police took the money and returned it to the car's owner." I cut my eyes to Axle who gave a double thumbs up.

When the man's ride pulled onto the shoulder, he climbed inside his buddy's car and the car's taillights disappeared down the road. I lifted my tired bod back into the truck and Axle climbed in the other side. We managed the entire tow without a word to each other—a woman and a wheelman in silent communication.

****

After dropping Axle at work the next morning, I fished Parker Smith's business card from the bottom of my purse.

"This is Parker Smith," he answered on the first ring. "Who's calling?"

"Delaney Morran."

"How can I help you?"

"Iceman was outside my apartment yesterday morning with two of his pals waiting for me. He was very threatening." *I know, I know*, I didn't tell Ephraim, but

Parker was the one who'd clued me in to Iceman in the first place. I promised not to bring the cops into the kidnapping, but I didn't promise not to alert drug enforcement about Iceman. I guess Courtnee's scary movies were still bothering me after all, plus reporting this threat to Parker eased my conscience a little.

"In what way?" His voice held some urgency.

I hedged, "He was trying for extortion. He wanted money." I couldn't go as far as to tell Parker about the kidnapping and ransom. For one thing, I didn't know how Iceman was involved. Let Parker grill it out of the dangerous gangster. "Are you going to question him?"

"We'll take it into consideration. Tell me exactly what was said."

After I recounted the conversation, without mentioning a kidnapping, he thanked me for calling and hung up.

I really should talk to Lance, too, but if I did would Lance threaten to whack Iceman? No way I would want to be responsible for that.

I made tracks to Roasters and joined the long queue for a coffee. The barista, Guy, took his time with my drink since I was the last one waiting. He handed me a double espresso with outstanding latte art in a tiny blue cup and mismatched green saucer. "You know those two old men who play chess all the time at the table in the corner? One of them lost his wife last week. And that man who plays video games in here, Roscoe? He was fired from his job."

"Wow, that's awful. How do you know all this?"

He chortled a laugh. "Your mom's been spending some time here. I'm surprised you haven't run into her."

"Oh, I've run into her." I ran a hand over my brow

feeling a headache coming on.

Guy said, "Kris is in the back if you want to say hello."

"I do." I skirted around the counter and made my way to her office.

She stared at her computer screen, tapping away at the keys. "What's up?"

"Mom stayed with me Saturday night."

Her eyes snapped up to mine. "She did?"

"Evidently you gave her a key."

"Uh…yes." Her face flushed. "What was I supposed to do? She asked me."

I tried to keep a reproachful look off my face. "Kris, her condo was infested with gnats. And I prayed for God to send her home, like you told me to. Were the bugs my fault? Did God send her a plague?"

"You actually prayed?"

"That's your takeaway? So not the point." My nervous hands pulled some strands from my thick braid. "You don't think God will send her more plagues, do you? Like making her hair fall out or something?"

"That wasn't one of the plagues." She flapped her hand in dismissal. "God wouldn't do that anyway."

"You always said God moves in mysterious ways."

"I didn't think you were listening to me." She looked thoughtful. "Maybe God wants you to get closer to your mom instead of pushing her away."

"I don't do that. And why do I need to get closer?"

"Because it's the right thing to do. Everything will work out for the best, you'll see." She appeared calm and serene as always. I wished my life was as even-keeled as Kristen's, with purpose and clarity, instead of stumbling around from one disaster to another, depending on luck and chance.

"I can only hope, Kris."

I made my way back to the front where coffee drinkers sat at tables dotted about the place. I downed my remaining espresso, set my cup in the dirty dish bin, and boosted myself out the door. My three-inch, razor-thin pink heels clip-clopped across the pavement. Pink for everything turning out rosy, my hope for today. I climbed in my truck and emerged out of the parking lot. The art gallery was empty of customers when I got there, but a smiling salesman, a large-framed man, appeared from a back room moments later.

"May I help you?"

I brought out a photo of Courtney that I'd downloaded from the internet. There were many to choose from since as an influencer she posted frequently on social media. And if I could figure all this out, I might be able to get Iceman off my mind and help Rory at the same time. "Do you know this woman?"

His smile dissolved; he probably realized I wasn't buying anything. "No, but I've seen her in the studio. Why?" He spoke with a marked lack of enthusiasm.

"I'm gathering information for a client."

"She was in here the other day, about a week ago."

"What was she looking at?" My eyes swept over the gallery full of mountain landscapes and horsey sculptures on pedestals. The air was stuffy from mothballs and dust motes.

"Mostly at her watch. She didn't purchase anything, just hung around like she was wasting time or waiting for someone."

"Did you happen to look in the alley out back?" I found myself crossing my fingers.

His nostrils pinched white. "Does this have to do with the car with the money and hand?"

"No, no." I blushed, thinking I just told a lie.

He took a second to respond, "You were the one who found the money."

"I didn't pocket any of it, I swear." I wagged my finger from side to side.

Defensive much?

He did an up and down thing with his eyes. "Is that all, then?"

"Yes." I double-timed it out the door.

Why did everyone choose to believe I would take money that didn't belong to me? And why does my guilt complex show itself when I'm innocent, of that anyway?

Quickly roaring my truck to life, I aimed toward Rory's house with the other mansions on the hill, but Rory wasn't home. No one answered the door, not even the housekeeper. I climbed back in my truck and thumbed my phone, searching my call history for Savanah's number, then hit the call button. "Are you still in town? Can we meet?" I asked after identifying myself.

"Yeah. My RV's at the house where Tanner towed me, directly across the street from Rory's."

"Just across the street, huh? I'm at Rory's house now." I stared at the ornate mailbox on the opposite side of the road, but I couldn't see the house hidden behind a stand of pines. I'd spotted James Atkins walking from that mailbox up the long curving driveway the other day. "Is Tanner with you?" I asked since she brought him up.

"No."

"I'll be there in a second. I have some questions for you." I dialed my stepdad Will since I'd intended to call him anyway. "Can you look up a property owner for me?

I just want verification. I want to know if the owner is James Atkins." I gave him the address on the mailbox.

"Hold on." He put me on mute. I stepped out onto the sidewalk and lifted my face toward a brilliant patch of blue sky that shone between the clouds, then I heard his voice as he unmuted. "You're right, James Atkins is listed as the property owner."

Not surprising. That Savanah's RV was parked at James' house was surprising, though, and helpful to know. Why in the world was her RV at Atkins' place? She'd been at his party, but how did they know each other? An older man and a young gal seemed suspect. He must like her to let her park an ugly RV on his beautiful grounds. It's really amazing how much property ownership information is available if you know where to find it. Public records were as handy as a winch on a truck, and having a lawyer in the family was convenient, too. I just hoped Will was still a part of my family.

"Have you talked to Mom yet?" I asked him.

"I left her a message."

"Will, have you tried calling her again?"

"The ball's in her court, Delaney."

"You two need to talk." I could hear him practically withdrawing over the connection. "Thanks for the information, Will." We both hung up.

The street was deserted except for a dogwalker and two goldendoodles on leashes. No road traffic, all was quiet. The wind was calm, but the scent of mulch and the whistling sound of hummingbirds infused the air. I followed the extended driveway through the tall trees. After what felt like a full city block, the house came into view, a yellow stucco monstrosity with three-story, white pillars flanking a ginormous door. Savanah's RV was set up in front of a triple garage. The RV's awning shaded two plastic chairs, and an extension cord snaked from the motor home to the house. The RV probably violated HOA rules, but the trees prevented it from being seen from the street.

Savanah slipped out the camper's door. "Hi, Del. What'd you want to talk to me about?"

"James' party a week ago." I nodded toward the mansion. "You were there, right?"

"Right."

"How do you know James?"

"I don't really. Or, I didn't know him before the party. I came to Spruce Ridge because I heard Rick Rearden was casting parts for a movie and that he was going to be at a party here. I crashed the party and met James. He's letting me camp out here for a few days."

"Why would he do that?" I really wanted to know, since they'd just met, as it turned out.

"He's a nice guy. Plus, I'm moving on shortly."

I returned to my original question, "About the party, how well do you know Rick Rearden?"

"Not very well. I hardly got to talk to him at all." She popped the camper door open as if to dodge back inside.

I had more questions and didn't want her to disappear out of sight. "Wait. There's a gang member who might've been hanging around here that night. His name is Iceman and he's dangerous. Do you know who I'm talking about?"

She clutched her throat. "He's dangerous?"

"I should say so." I gave her a *duh-don't be stupid* look. "With a name like Iceman."

"Really? I thought his name was, like, from the

movie *Top Gun*."

"You've seen him around?"

"I don't know…maybe?" She splayed a hand across her chest. "I mostly see dead people." She gave me a wink.

"You know him though?"

"Yeah, I know who he is."

The sound of tires on cement caused us to spin around. A Subaru Outback, all-wheel drive, rocked to a stop and Wyatt Tagert, the tabloid photographer, got out with a camera hanging from his shoulder.

"What are you doing here?" I asked him.

"I'm here to talk to Savanah." He gave her a smile.

She laughed. "He's not really here for me. He wants photos of Rickney."

Wyatt said, "And I can't seem to get any pictures of them together lately."

"Who's Rickney?" I asked.

"Don't you read *Muckamuck Magazine*?" She gave me an eyeroll.

"Never heard of it."

Both Savanah and Wyatt gasped. Savanah said, "Well, you should read it. Rick and Courtney as a couple spells Rickney."

"Who are you and what are you doing on my property?" A man's aggravated voice caused us to spin in the other direction.

James Atkins came pelting toward us, bouncing glances between me and Wyatt Tagert. I stared at the man, not sure what to say, and no words came out of Wyatt's mouth either.

"Hello, James. This is Delaney Morran." Savanah reached out to squeeze my elbow. "And this is Wyatt

Tagert with *Muckamuck Magazine*." The photographer lifted his professional-sized camera as if to show James, then he swiveled to the right and shot a picture of the mansion.

James' face tightened. "None of that. Delete that photo." Wyatt clutched his camera to his chest. "I mean it. Now. You are on my property without permission and I can call the police."

"All right, all right." Wyatt deleted the photo and showed James his screen to prove it.

"You were hanging around my party, too. I suppose you got a ton of pictures, you slimy weasel."

Wyatt said, "You know I didn't get any. Your muscle ran me off."

James flung his hand toward the Subaru. "He had the right idea. Get out of here."

Wyatt took his time leaning down to get in his car, and a long moment passed before he reversed down the drive.

"What'd you do that for, James?" Savanah gave him a pout. "Wyatt was only doing his job."

"I have a right to my privacy. No one needs to know my business."

"He was only taking a picture outside."

"Outside, now. Drone over the pool, later. All to be splashed on the front page of *Muckamuck*." James' head whipped in my direction like I was next to be warned off.

I squeaked out, "Remember me? We met at Rory's house the other day."

He dismissed me with a nod. "Savanah, if you see anyone lurking around, be sure to let me know."

"I will, James, but everything's fine out here." She cast a glance at her motorhome. The RV's louvered windows were shuttered and the truck's front windshield was obscured by a sun-blocking visor. The camper door remained closed tight.

James gave me a final glare before he retreated inside the house.

Once he was gone, I asked Savanah, "What was that about?"

She admitted in a small voice, "I should probably move my RV soon. James is particular about his privacy."

"Why are you here?"

"I still have a few things to take care of before I leave for California."

"Tanner said you have a job lined up in Hollywood."

Her face brightened. "Did he say he was coming with me?"

I gave her a cold look. "No. Tanner has responsibilities here in Spruce Ridge. He would never leave his family."

She shook her head. "We'll see about that. May the force be with you." She cracked the RV door open and wriggled inside before clicking it shut after her. As I retreated down the long, curved driveway, I felt an odd prickling at the back of my neck and thought she may be watching me from inside her camper.

Wyatt was waiting at my tow truck. "Strange, isn't it?" he asked.

"Yeah, James was a little cheesed off." I strode up to the door of my truck and beeped the fob.

"No, I mean that Rick Rearden's not around. My sources tell me he's not on location. I haven't seen him here, either. Where is he?" When I shrugged, he asked, "If you see Rick, and especially if you see Courtney and

Rick together, will you call me?"

"I've never met Rick, and Courtney doesn't even like me. I don't understand why the public is fascinated with them."

"They're the hot topic 'cause they're a train wreck, always fighting in public. Courtney really should listen to her manager and quit with her nasty on-line posts, but her fans love it. She gets a ton of views."

I scrunched my forehead. "Yeah, what are those about?"

"Publicity. She's an influencer, you know."

"*Okaay*," I drew the word out. "I wonder why James invited them to his party. He seems so private, like he wouldn't want the publicity, and I heard Courtney and Rick argued at his house."

Wyatt's eyes gleamed. "What did they argue about?"

"I don't know. I wasn't there, but you were. What did you see?"

"I missed that. James' thug forced me off the property almost as soon as I got there."

"Why does James let Savanah park in his driveway, if he's so particular?"

"I don't know, but once you're in with these people, you're in." There was a wistful sound to his voice.

I pounced on that. "Who is Savanah friends with?"

"Well, she was hanging with Rick at the party for a little while, but that doesn't mean much. A lot of women hang around Rick. He's a babe magnet, being a movie producer."

"Didn't you get any photos? Not even one?"

"I did get a few, but there was nothing I could use."

"Can I see them?"

We leaned against my tow truck, side-by-side, while Wyatt searched through his camera viewfinder, swiping through photos. Then he angled the lens for me to see as he thumbed past a few more.

"Stop there." A group photo with Parker Smith in the background opened up. Parker was in a tee-shirt and sloppy jeans, and reflector sunglasses covered his face—possibly his undercover look—but I still recognized him. "Do you know that man?"

Wyatt said, "No. Who is he?" When I just shrugged, he handed me his card. "Here's my number. If you see Rick and Courtney together, you'll call me, won't you?" He didn't wait for my answer before setting off at a brisk pace toward his Subaru.

When I walked into my apartment, I was hit with the cheesy smell of home cooking and figured Axle had one of Mom's casseroles in the oven. I called out, "Hey, Axle, you home?"

He swung down the hall from his room and almost plowed over me on his way to the oven. "Dinner's almost ready thanks to your mom."

While I set the table, he fed his furry baby and made sure Boss's water bowl was fresh. We happily munched until the last bite disappeared and we pushed our plates away. I patted my stomach and burped. Mom's casseroles were killing me.

I asked, "How's the work on your car coming along?" He was constantly overhauling his used Nissan Altima, front-wheel drive.

"I'll have her put back together soon." He brought the dirty dishes to the sink. "Why? You tired of driving me around?"

"No." I scraped and rinsed the plates. "I don't

mind."

"We all good in the hood?"

"'Course." I loaded the plates and turned on the dishwasher, then stood and stretched, cracking my back. Boss, finally aware the food was gone, took a sloppy drink from his water bowl. "Are you up for some surveillance?"

"Staking out a repo?"

"A kidnapper." I raised my eyebrows up and down several times.

A know-it-all grin broke out on his face. "Let's get the party started."

Chapter 13

Above the mountain peaks, the night-time sky glowed with pink and orange streaks, and everywhere else had faded to black. The neighborhood was dark and silent except for the Fiat's ticking engine as it cooled. Wanting out, Boss whined from the backseat.

"We probably shouldn't have brought your dog with us." I squirmed when the Rotty licked my ear and drooled on my neck.

"He's good cover. We can walk him around and get a little closer. It's hard to see the house in the dark with all these trees." He cracked open his door. "Let's air out."

Boss jumped down after him and wiggled with excitement, happy to be released from the Fiat. Axle clamped the leash to his collar and the three of us crept down the sidewalk where halogen streetlights made circles of artificial light. Boss stretched up his muzzle and sniffed the air, then proceeded to sprinkle every bush along the way. The Rottweiler lost interest in that, so we veered up the driveway and once we got around the curve, we put on some speed. Lights shone from the colossal windows dominating the front of James Atkin's stucco mansion, but that didn't mean he was home. Some millionaires didn't worry about their electric bill or their carbon footprint. In contrast, the yellow-striped RV with its louvered windows was cloaked in darkness.

No one came out of the house. No one appeared in the windows. No vehicles drove down the street. Savanah didn't stir from her camper, either.

"Not much to see," Axle said, voicing my exact opinion.

We returned to the Fiat and settled into our seats to wait some more.

"Ax, there's something I haven't told you."

"Spill."

"You know the severed hand? Well, now there's a foot, too. A foot was sent to Rory's aunt. It could be her husband's." I'd been about to burst with this secret since Axle and Lance are the only people I'd told about the kidnapping. I hadn't told the sheriff. Hadn't told the drug agent. Hadn't even told Kristen. Sometimes I amazed myself.

His eyes bugged out. "Good story."

"Thanks. I wish it weren't true."

"This is getting out of hand."

I started to agree, then he gave me a superior smile, so I buddy-punched him in the arm. I anticipated him making a joke; I didn't guess he'd make that one. "Courtney delivered the money to the kidnapper, but her husband wasn't released. It's possible he's dead. Lance and I were with her at the drop-off. Rory, too."

"Whoa. Really?" He lowered his window and Boss thrust his head through, panting.

I blurted out the whole account, including my mom showing up at the Park-n-Ride and Iceman showing up the next morning to ask me about the money. As if I had it.

"That sucks." He was able to knock his shoulder against mine in my tiny Fiat.

"Damn straight."

"You tell Lopez about this?"

"No, but I did tell that drug agent, Parker Smith, about Iceman. But not about the kidnapping or anything else." I'd been on high-alert, although Iceman had not made another appearance around our apartment, nor had I spotted him or his car anywhere else. "If Iceman's the kidnapper, he wasn't the one to pick up the ransom, otherwise why would he ask me where the money is?"

"Iceman sent someone else to the drop-off, and that person took off with the cash."

"I had that same thought."

"Tell me, again, why we're here."

"This is where the party was. Rick disappeared from here. James doesn't want anyone nosing around. Why's that?" On edge, I craned my neck every which way, and it seemed we were alone, but my nerves made me feel as exposed as the tread on a bald tire. "I can't sit still. Let's take Boss for another walk, and if we still don't see anything, we can leave."

"I knew you had a plan."

We shouldered open the car doors and met at the curb. Boss must've forgotten he'd marked all the bushes already because he set out to do it again. Rock crunched under my heels as I stepped off the sidewalk into the landscaping. Axle followed me into the bushes, and Boss followed him. After letting my eyes adjust to the dark, I extracted a pair of tiny binoculars and we took turns scoping out the massive, uncovered windows.

"What should we be looking for?" I asked my lil' cuz'.

"Saws. Big knives. Blood. A headless corpse."

"Nope," I said. "Don't see any of those things."

Somewhere a twig cracked and my flesh crawled. It was probably just Boss, whose nose was buried in the underbrush.

Sirens whooped from a not-too-far distance, and we hurried toward the street, Boss in the lead. The windows in Rory's house were lit like beacons, illuminating a car parked in the circular driveway, a gray Ford Fusion hybrid, front-wheel drive. A man in a gray suit cracked the driver's door open, slid out, and silently shut the door behind him. He slunk around the corner in the direction of the guest cottage.

I whispered to keep my voice low, "That was Parker Smith. The narcotics agent I was telling you about." Axle gave me an unconcerned shrug.

The police sirens grew closer in that indiscernible way, as if the sound was coming from every direction. The *woo-wee-woo-wee* escalated until our ears were about to burst. Was there a domestic disturbance? An armed robbery in progress? A cat burglar? A cop car careened down the street and screeched to a halt, blinding us with its headlights and strobes flashing against the curb. Boss exploded into barking and strained at his leash. I had an apple-sized lump of panic in my throat, making it feel swollen to twice its size.

I dropped the leash and ran screaming for the Fiat. Okay, so I was a little freaked.

A uniformed policeman climbed out of the cruiser. "Delaney, is that you?"

"Y-y-yes?" I crouched next to my car, my whole body tensed, and held my hand up to shield my eyes from the glare. Boss trotted over to give the officer's hand a lick. I asked, "Zach?"

He shut off the siren and the quiet of the night

returned. He bobbed a flashlight in our direction. "The neighborhood watch group reported a possible prowler."

I rose to a stand. "*Omigosh*! Where?"

"Well, what are you doing here?" Zach pinched his eyebrows together.

"Us?" My voice only cracked a little.

"We're just taking Boss for a walk," Axle said. He still stood on the sidewalk, and Boss had returned to sit at his feet.

"Why here?"

I said, "Rory lives across the street." I lacked a better answer and stared at the officer to see if he was buying it.

Apparently he did. "Okay. I'll call it in, no assistance needed."

"Why did you have your sirens on? Don't you like to sneak up on criminals?"

"I was exceeding the limit. When responding at speed we use a yelp siren."

"'K. Well, we're out of here. See you later, Zach." I hopped inside my car, and Axle climbed in with Boss bounding in after him.

"Good one, Delaney," Axle said as he fastened his seatbelt.

"I know, he believed our story."

"No, that's not it. I'm being sarcastic. You almost got us arrested."

"How was that my fault?"

He stared out the window, blew out a breath, then glanced back at me. "Your idea."

"Well, yeah, that part, but you went along with it." I bit back any further retort. Maybe because he was right. "What was Parker Smith doing creeping around Rory's house?" I asked him.

"Maybe he's the prowler. You should have told Zach about him."

"Parker's an undercover drug investigator, not a prowler, but maybe I should have. What do you think he was doing there?"

"Undercover work, like you said."

"Hmmm." I wondered about that for a moment and went over the curb at the corner since I wasn't paying attention.

"Stick to the pavement, dude." Axle popped in an earbud to listen to his tunes while I retraced the route home.

****

The next day stretched into evening. As it was Tuesday night, I slowly weaved my truck up and down the rutted alleyways behind the tow-away zones. A Honda Civic, front-wheel drive, was blocking the furniture company's loading dock, and I idled at its rear bumper for a few minutes. A man, in his sixties or so, wearing brown dress pants and a button-down shirt, trudged down the alley toward the Civic, and I watched to see whether it was his car.

He approached my driver's side. He said, "So, you're a tow truck driver," and laughed. "Sorry. I've never seen a female tow truck driver before."

"I'm Delaney Morran of Del's Towing." I revved my truck's engine.

"You're the one—"

"—Yeah, yeah, that was me. No, I didn't take any of the money. I'm an honest female tow truck driver."

"I wasn't going to say that. I was going to say, aren't you the one who wears high heels? Aren't you the high-heeled tow truck driver?"

"You saw the logo." I gave him a quick smile, my stacked denim heels hidden from his sight. Denim for being casual tonight. "If this is your Honda you need to move it now."

"Sure thing. Have a nice evening." He reversed and exited the alley, once I was out of his way.

I moved to the next block and managed to coax my big truck into a tight space alongside the dumpster before shutting off the ignition. The glare from the spotlight on the back of the building threw deep shadows, making my truck almost invisible. Since the night was warm, I rolled down the window to let the fresh air inside. Big mistake. Hello, dumpster. Not empty this time. A rotting meat stench filled my sinuses, and I powered the window up again.

I cast my gaze over the backstreet, taking in a final sweep of my surroundings, when I noticed a raggedy gym shoe attached to a dirty, jean-clad leg behind the dumpster. Likely a homeless person who just wanted to be left alone, but since he could be injured or sick, I forced myself out of the truck and made my way around the corner of the large metal bin. And there it was. The rotting smell. The reeking body of a dead man.

Missing a right hand.

And a right foot.

With a stink that could take down a grizzly.

His body faced down. The back of his jeans and tee shirt were caked with dried blood. His head was shaved and his upper arms were as wide as my thighs, like a weightlifter. I did a deep knee bend to get a closer look and gagged on the smell. I didn't turn him over; I knew better than that. Rick Rearden didn't have a shaved head or such muscular arms, at least not in any of the photos I'd seen, so this was not him. Part of me was relieved the dismembered hand and foot didn't belong to Rick. They belonged to this guy.

I ripped out my cell phone and punched in Ephraim's number. "I found a dead man in the alley behind Main Street Coffee Shop. He's missing a hand and foot." I batted away flies that buzzed around my head.

Ephraim told me to get back in my truck and lock the doors, then said I was to stay on the phone until the sheriff cruisers arrived. The thought of danger hadn't crossed my mind, but I wasn't thinking straight. Not because of a killer, but because of the scary vibes from a mutilated body.

I ran for my truck and slammed down the locks. The shadows looked darker and the alley emptier than ever before. What seemed forever, but was only moments later, Ephraim's truck zoomed into the alley along with three other sheriff's cruisers. He scrambled out of his pickup and veered right over to me.

"Are you okay?"

"I'm fine. Go do what you need to do," I said. Ephraim nodded, then left me in my truck to join the other officers around the corpse.

To be honest, I wasn't fine. Only minutes had passed since my discovery, and the shaky feeling was still with me. I had to talk to somebody, so I called Kristen and told her all about it. She got off the phone to call Zach, so I dialed up Tanner, who needed to know since it was his contract to monitor the tow-away zones. Tanner said he was on his way and hung up. I called Axle next. He wanted to come right over, too, but I told him not to, and he didn't have a ride anyway. Then I called Lance Palmero and left a message. I guess my motor mouth was running at top speed because of my shot nerves and not wanting to be alone in my truck.

While I was busy staring out my windshield, Lance rapped his knuckles on the passenger window. I opened the door from the inside and he angled himself into the cab.

His face pointed at me. "This is Iceman's mark."

"That's what I thought, too." My chin quivered. "It's his territory now, right?"

"He thinks so. He wants to be the high roller. But you're safe. You're okay 'cause you got me. I'm your back up, your main man."

"I don't want to upset you, Lance, but…" I clasped my hands together to keep them from trembling. "…I think Iceman planted this body in the alley so I would find it. He knows where I live because he showed up there. He probably knows I work back here, too."

"Iceman showed up at your digs?"

"He did. He asked me if I knew where the ransom money is. Do you still think he's the kidnapper?"

He jerked his head toward the dead guy. "Look at the proof." Lance's lips clenched together in a tight line and we sat in silence for a while.

I asked him, "Do you know the victim? Did you get a look at him?"

"No. I didn't go over there near them cops." He rubbed his lightning bolt tattoo and a deep frown settled on his face.

A gray Ford Fusion hybrid, front-wheel drive, pulled in behind the cop cars. Parker Smith, in a suit and loosened tie, folded himself out of the driver's seat. He greeted Ephraim and became absorbed in their circle around the crime scene.

"Lance, that guy is with the Denver Drug Task Force. He always seems to be around, showing up everywhere."

"Yeah, he looks like *21 Jump Street*." The gangster stuck a cigarette between his lips but didn't light it, then he stretched his long legs out, taking up all the space in the truck cab.

"He was at James' party, undercover. Did you see him?"

"Maybe. Was he wearing glasses?"

"Yeah, he was. He said he was after Iceman, but I have another theory." I sat up straighter and turned in my seat to face Lance. "Smith is on the inside, right? So he's in a perfect position to frame somebody. What if he killed that man over there and made it look like a gang slaying? He could be the kidnapper, too."

"What would he get out of it?"

"Eliminate Rick Rearden, a drug user who's a big spender, get rid of that guy, whoever he is," I waved a finger toward the body, "and bust the head of the new gang in town, all at the same time."

"Could be, could be." He drew a bead on Parker Smith, then stole a glance my way. "Gotta book. I'll see you later." He silently swung open the passenger door and melted away into the dark alley.

The owner of Main Street Coffee, Mike Horn, turned his distinctive Mazda Miata roadster, rear-wheel drive, into the alley, and right after him Tanner showed up in his black Volvo S60, front-wheel drive, not in his tow truck tonight. Tanner and Mike got out of their vehicles and met at the coffee shop's loading dock, and

I was just about to leave my truck and join them, when Ephraim strode over.

He asked, "What were you doing talking to Lance Palmero? You should've given us your statement before speaking to anyone else, especially him." Not a single muscle moved on his face. He was in cop mode.

"I called him."

"Hang on. You called him?" Red crept up his neck.

I lifted my palms. "That's what I said."

"It's possible Lance Palmero knew the victim. Palmero could be a suspect here. Do you want to get swept up in a dangerous situation again, like what happened at the drug raid at the cowboy bar?"

"No."

"We're going to pick him up for questioning."

"You let him leave."

"We know where he lives. Interesting that he showed up at the crime scene."

"That's because I called him, like I told you."

Ephraim eyed the seat just vacated by gangster with distaste, like he didn't want to share the same oxygen with the man. "I want you to get in the sheriff's cruiser so we can talk."

I hesitated, but it sounded more like an order than a request, so I followed him to his four-door Chevy Silverado pickup with *Sheriff - Clear Creek County* painted black on white.

Once we were shut inside together, I asked, "Did you get an ID on the body?"

Ephraim's face was in deep shadows. "The victim's name is Jack Wojcik. Does that mean anything to you?"

"No."

"Ever see him before?"

"I didn't get a look at his face. Do you need me to?" I gave an involuntary shudder and pressed a hand to my mouth.

He leaned toward me, his face suddenly in the light, his gaze burdened and troubled. "No, of course not." He reached into the backseat and grabbed a clipboard. "Fill out this witness statement for me."

I took the clipboard, blinking back the annoying water in my eyes, filled out the form, and handed it to him. "I'd like to leave now."

"You can go."

First I had to ask, "How was that man killed?"

"Stabbed."

"Was he dead before the hand and foot were chopped off?"

"The coroner needs to make that determination, Delaney." When he saw my shocked face, he added, "Probably."

"How did you identify him so quickly?"

"The victim's well known to us." He sat back in his seat and crossed his arms. "I want you to stay away from Palmero. Can you do that for me?"

I gathered the strands of my long curly hair together then let them go again. "Since it's you asking, I'll think about it."

"Do more than think about it."

I turned my face away from him, causing the air between us to thicken with tension and words unsaid. No doubt, Lance Palmero was dangerous, even if he told me we were fellow Thunder Knuckles gang members. Lance may have said it, but *no way* was I a gang member. It was crazy to consider the idea. I had no business getting involved in any of this. I should step away. None of this has anything to do with me or my job. My job is simple. Tow cars. Collect fees. Release cars to owners. Period. Ephraim would deal with the body and the evident drug war that was going on; I could leave it all behind.

"All right," I conceded.

"Good." His brown eyes softened as he pulled me to him across the console and rubbed my back. "Are you still mad at me?"

I poked the air. "Yes."

"But why?"

His height forced me to tilt my head to look up at him. "The blonde." *Duh*.

He gave me the thousand yard stare. "I don't know who you're talking about."

Were we really going to have this conversation right now? In a police vehicle? Next to a dead body? Not very romantic, plus his denial only pissed me off.

A camera flash lit up the front seat, and we shoved apart.

"Oh hell." Ephraim ran a hand down his face. He wrenched his door open. "You, there. You can't take pictures." He grabbed the man's camera, and that's when I recognized the photographer, Wyatt Tagert, who'd been trying to track down Courtney and Rick, or as they say, Rickney. Was he following me, too, or did he see the crowd and swoop in for the latest news?

I boosted myself from Ephraim's truck to eavesdrop.

Wyatt said, "Sorry, Sheriff, but I'm a member of the press."

"This is an active crime scene, you need to step back. A press release will be posted later." Ephraim walked him down the alley until he and Wyatt passed out of view. Ephraim ambled back, several officers motioned him over, and I heard Ephraim tell them, "Check the dumpsters and the perimeter for the foot. I think I know where the hand is."

Time for me to get out of here. I quick-stepped to my truck and eased it out from alongside the dumpster. As I rolled past Tanner and Horn, they waved at me but I kept going.

I hadn't admitted this to Ephraim or myself, and my throat tightened at the memory, but something looked familiar about the body. Not just the missing hand and foot part, either. Somehow I felt I should've recognized the victim, even though I hadn't caught a glimpse of his face. And why did I have to be the one to find the body? Why me? Had Iceman set me up like I suspected? Or was I just unlucky? So many things in my life seemed to result from a twist of fate.

Another thing weighed on my chest…I didn't tell Ephraim where to find the severed foot. I kept telling myself the foot didn't matter. Yeah, I know it does matter. I was only fooling myself.

****

The next morning, exhausted from a long night of head-spinning playbacks of the awful scene, I came out to the kitchen to find a note from Axle that he had the day off and not to wake him. Instead of my usual routine of a Roasters on the Ridge espresso and a drive to retrieve my tow truck, I made a beeline for Main Street Coffee. Mike Horn might've heard something after I left the scene last night. I'd talk to Tanner later, since he'd shown up as well, but right now I could find out what Mike knew and get my caffeine fix on, too. *Win, win.*

The café was in a historical building, but instead of

an old-timey, western atmosphere, the place had an old-world, European feel, with booths in the mid-century modern style and brightly colored upholstery next to the floor-to-ceiling windows. Perfect seating to watch all the pedestrians pass by. Two teens sat sipping lattes at one table. At another, a young mom wiggled a baby stroller by her side. At a third, the drug agent, Parker Smith, sat speaking quietly with two other men I knew. I stared at them as I made my way to the counter, my head staying pointed in their direction.

Mike greeted me. "Why there's little Delaney. Little Laney. You're looking fine this morning," he said in his flirty way.

"Good morning." I gestured toward Parker's table. "Do you know those men?"

"No."

Hard to believe, since these three seemed to be bigshots in this small town. I said, "One of them is Rory's dad, Randy Rearden. You don't know him?"

"Can't say I do."

"How about James Atkins? Parker Smith? Ever heard of them?" I cast a glance over my shoulder but couldn't catch any of their words. Randy Rearden, James Atkins, and Parker Smith spoke in low voices. Parker seemed to be leading the conversation.

Mike said, "No. You want a coffee?"

"Are tires round? Of course I do. Violet knows my order."

He signaled to Violet behind the espresso machine.

"So, Mike, what happened last night after I left? Did you find out anything? You know, about the body…" I rolled my eyes in the direction of the back of the building toward the alley, then I sneaked another peek at the three men at the table.

"The cops asked me if I'd seen the dead man hanging around. I guess they thought since his body was found near my dumpster that I might've seen him before, but I hadn't." Mike shook his head fiercely. "He wasn't anyone I knew."

"Here you go." Violet pushed a double espresso into my hands.

"Thanks." I took a sip through the to-go lid and scalded my tongue. "You got a look at his face?" I asked Mike.

"Yeah. I didn't recognize him." He moved his head side to side. "The cops gave me his name, Jack Wojcik, but I never heard of him."

Note to self: find out who Wojcik is.

A chair screeched behind me and I swung around. Parker had gotten up from his table, and he said loud enough for me to hear, "I don't have any more questions at this time."

James stood. "If you do, call my attorney." He looked over at Randy, who also rose from his seat, and all three went out the door. If I hadn't guessed it before, I knew now that Parker Smith was interrogating James and Randy. Was Randy at James' party, too? Rory hadn't mentioned that his dad was there, and you'd think he would have. Randy seemed to be friends with James. Were they more than just neighbors? Did they hang out together? Or do business together?

I watched until the door closed after the three of them, then turned back to Mike. "Did the police question Tanner? I called him last night to let him know what happened, but I didn't know he was going to show up."

"Yeah. Tanner had a look at the body, too, but he

had no idea who the guy was, either. How about you?"

"I never saw his face." I *had* seen him before, though. But where?

Chapter 14

Pine Street was heavy with traffic when I stopped my Fiat at the light. A man and a woman cycled in the bike lane toward the river. Runners in jogging gear and shoppers with bags cleared the crosswalk before the light turned green. I made the corner at the mall and slid into a parking space under a shade tree.

After debating for a moment or two, I sneaked past the makeup counter to spy on Ephraim's blonde—she wasn't there. So I ran inside the discount shoe store instead and looked over the sales rack. And tried on a few pair. And purchased leather fisherman sandals with chunky heels. *Adorbs!* But a new pair of shoes would go a long way to keeping me upbeat about that blonde Ephraim denied knowing. Or Mom's housewarming party that started half an hour ago. I couldn't delay any longer; I'd better get over there.

Procrastinate, much?

The elevator in Mom's condo whisked me up to the seventh floor. The window at the end of the corridor displayed an unobstructed view of the Rocky Mountains. Off in the distance, undulating peaks in shades of purple and blue pierced the sky. Closer in, the sight of verdant aspen, mint-colored sagebrush, and brown, old-growth pines made my heart soar and my world feel large and at peace. I could see why Mom liked this place.

When I turned the knob and entered, I expected two

or three ladies from Mom's social group sampling wine and cheese. I didn't anticipate this crush of people. Or these people. Tanner chatted with Kristen and Zach; Axle and Shannon scooped food onto plates; Byron talked with Guy from Kristen's coffee shop; Courtney was taking selfies on her phone while giving the photographer, Wyatt, the evil eye; and James and Savanah arrived at the door after me. Just about everyone I knew in this town was here.

Mom spotted me and hustled over. "I'm glad you made it, Laney. Do you want a glass of wine? Some cheese?" At least the wine and cheese were as I expected.

After a moment of astonished silence, I asked, "Mom, why'd you invite all my friends?"

"You know I've always liked your friends."

"Courtney Rearden?"

Her eyes lit up. "You know she's in the movies?"

"What about that guy over there? How do you know him?" It looked to me like the photographer was trying to sneak pictures of Courtney during her selfie-session.

"Oh, Wyatt's always hanging around Roasters, and he knows all the gossip about celebrities. I just had to invite him. Speaking of gossip, I heard something about you." She clasped my arm so tightly it pinched.

"What?" I tried not to have a *deer-in-the-headlights* look.

"You found a dead body last night. And you found bags of cash, millions of dollars, in the backseat of a car, too. Are you mixed up in something dangerous?"

"It wasn't millions of dollars."

"Who do you think did it? Don't tell me the killer is here." Her voice was strained.

We both took a quick look around the room. More

of my friends had showed up at Mom's than at my place the last time I had a get-together. A burst of laughter from the corner caught her attention, and she said, "I'll be back," before making a straight line in that direction.

I was rubbing my temples when Kristen came up and shoved a glass of wine in my hand. "You probably need this."

"You're probably right." I snatched the glass from her grip.

Mom held up a champagne flute and tapped a fork on the side, making a ting-a-ling sound. "Everyone, I have an announcement." Was Mom about to pull a Hercule Poirot, having gathered all the suspects together to reveal the murderer?

I whispered to Kris from the side of my mouth, "Mom has taken over my apartment, taken over my friends, and now she's taken over my investigation, too."

"What do you mean?"

"She does my laundry and grocery shopping. She cleans my apartment."

"Is that a bad thing? And what do you mean, your investigation?"

"Look around."

Iceman was the only suspect missing. At least she hadn't invited him.

"Listen up." Mom hoisted her glass. "Thanks everyone for helping me celebrate my new place."

There were several, "Hear-hears," and "Congratulations," before everyone took a sip from their glasses, then resumed their conversations.

The food-laden table drew me over: cheese tray, chips and guacamole, and mini Mexican quiches covered with green chili. Everything in Colorado comes with green chili. Having lived here all my life, I loved the spicy topping and prepared a small plate for myself.

Mom was making her rounds again, and when she edged past me I stopped her. "Have you talked to Will?"

Her face fell a little. "Don't spoil my moment, Laney."

I forced a smile. "All right, but you two need to talk."

"You should go over and speak to Tanner." She gave me a pointed look.

"Why should I do that?"

"Because he likes you and he's such a nice man. After all, you aren't going out with the sheriff anymore."

"Have you been talking to Tanner?"

"Yes. We had a nice chat before you got here, but I heard that bit of news about you from Wyatt."

Wyatt! *Argh!* Could this get any worse? No, just no.

She flitted away and started going from one group to another like a hummingbird, so I tracked down Axle.

I said to him, "So, you're here, too."

"What can I say? Your mom can cook and the party's *kewl*." He crammed a mini quiche into his mouth, chewed, and swallowed. "She asked me for the phone numbers of your friends, and I invited Byron and a few of the guys, too." He pointed his chin to the kitchen where three auto mechanics from L&B Garage were looking in the fridge, probably for beer.

"Oh my God, Axle. You owe me one." I gave him a sharp elbow to his ribs, then took a bite of my own quiche.

"Yeah, yeah, deal with it," Axle sputtered, crumbs spilling out of his mouth.

Tanner slouched with crossed arms against the wall

near a high-top bistro table covered with tiered dessert trays. A yummy cupcake called to me—and I'm not talking about Tanner, whose slim build hid serious muscles and a washboard abdomen from hard physical labor. His blond hair had that tousled look I knew was natural and not the result of hair gel and time spent in front of the mirror. He was alone, so it didn't look like he'd brought a date. Savanah had arrived with James, I noted. I suddenly realized Tanner had caught me staring at him, and I got a rush when he walked up to me.

"Hey, Tanner. That stank last night, *amiright?*"

"Yeah."

"Did the cops question you?" I plucked a cupcake from the dessert tray.

"They asked me if I knew the guy, Jack Wojcik. I didn't recognize him." Tanner's cellphone buzzed and he checked the screen. "Call for a tow. I'm outta here."

"Oh, that's too bad. These cupcakes are great. You should take food with you." I tried to hide my disappointment.

"I ate one already. Tell your mom goodbye for me."

I got one more glance at him before he went out the door and I searched the crowd for James and Savanah, but they must've left after making a short appearance. Once I'd finished the cupcake and thrown my paper plate into the trash, I made my way over to Rory's aunt. She looked up when I stopped in front of her at the picture window. Mom's view was even better than the one in the hall.

"No word?" I kept my voice low.

"Nothing. I was so sure they'd call." She frowned and fiddled with her phone.

"Did you hear about the body in the alley behind

Main? Severed foot and hand?" I raised my eyebrows.

Courtney nodded. "The sheriff called and questioned me about it, like I'd know anything. Do you know who the victim was? The sheriff didn't give me any information, other than his name, Jack Wojcik."

"The name didn't sound familiar?"

She shook her head. No one seemed to know him.

"I don't suppose you told Ephraim about the foot?" I asked.

"No! No, no, no, and you'd better not, either," Courtney insisted, then looked around to make sure no one heard her, but loud voices and occasional coughs had covered her words.

"Since I was the one who found the body, I think I should have a say in this," I complained.

Courtney made a pouty face at me, then held up her cellphone to capture the look in a photo, with the view out the window in the background. I stared at her as she made other faces, happy with a wide smile, then sad with a teary look, while snapping more pictures. She really wasn't a bad actress.

When her fingers got busy tapping on her phone, I asked, "What are you doing?"

"Posting on social media."

"Why do you broadcast pictures of yourself when you don't like the paparazzi taking your photo?"

"I told you before, I make money with sponsored posts. Why should I let *Muckamuck Magazine* make money off of me? Videos of me arguing with Rick in public places go viral." She laughed.

"Is that why you post complaints about your husband?"

She lifted her shoulder and let it fall without taking

her eyes off her phone screen. What would happen to her marketing scheme if Rick's abduction were discovered? Or if something worse happened to him? Would her profits decrease or double?

After a while, Courtney, looking bored, took off, and the other guests started trickling out of the condo, so I carted a few empty platters to the kitchen. I filled the sink with soapy water to soak the pans while Mom refilled the remaining guests' wine glasses and encouraged everyone to have seconds. Once the last person departed, Mom and I slouched onto her white sofa, amazingly still pristine.

"This is a nice place, Mom. Nice view."

"Thanks. Did you get new shoes? They're real cute." Mom rubbed her fingers across her eyelids.

"You're worn out, putting on a big party like this." I leaned forward and grasped both her hands in mine. "Did you at least invite Will?"

She slid out of my hold. "No."

"Come on, Mom. You need to forgive him sometime. He's sorry this happened, you know." This wasn't exactly a lie, I'm almost certain.

She said, "Don't worry about it," followed by an obvious *mind-your-own-business* look. What could I say to that? "Let's put the leftovers away."

I clasped my knees to stand up. We worked together in the kitchen, then I ran the vacuum while Mom wiped the table and lined up all the couch cushions.

"Need anything else?" I offered before heading out.

She handed me a bag of leftovers. "Thanks for everything, Laney. I love you so much. You be careful, you hear?" Her eyes misted up, and my eyes drew damp, too. I felt funny leaving her all alone.

I needed to fix this thing between Mom and Will, but how?

Stepping outside the condo, I opened Will's contact on my phone screen, but after remembering Mom's face, I closed that and hit Lance Palmero's number instead.

"Yo," he said by way of greeting.

"Any news?" I squished the phone against my shoulder and threw my purse in my Fiat before climbing inside.

"Nuthin'." He drew a deep breath then blurted out, "Come to the baseball game with me. I got good tickets."

"When?"

"Today. I'm already down here for the pre-game shows at the bars."

"Well…" It was an hour's drive to Denver.

"Game doesn't start till four." Lance urged me, "We need to check it out. I got word Iceman's gonna show."

"He is?" If I was looking for an excuse to go, here it was. But how stupid could I be? I told Ephraim I wouldn't spend time with Lance.

Lance said, "Come on, Del."

Was I actually thinking about going? Of course. How could I pass up this opportunity? Iceman was going to be there. Maybe James Atkins would be there, too, since—according to Rory—he supplied the food trucks outside the stadium, and I could talk to him. I hadn't gotten a chance at Mom's party because James hadn't stuck around. Likely he needed to make sure his trucks were at the game. Maybe I would even see James and Iceman there together. Yeah, I was having a hard time believing I'd be that lucky, but I clamped down all thoughts of Ephraim and made a quick decision. The sheriff hadn't told me much about his investigation, so I might as well keep asking questions of my own.

"I'll meet you there." I turned the key to fire up the Fiat, then zipped my little Italian job down to Denver in what seemed like no time at all.

Lance stood at the corner of 20th and Blake near the food trucks, and I approached him from the parking lot across the street. The gangster wore a baseball hat at a right angle as his only concession to fanhood. The lightning bolt on his forehead peeped out from under the sideways ball cap, and silver lightning bolt earrings dangled from his lobes. The man's pants bagged low on his hips. Between his thumb and forefinger he clinched an unlit cigarette.

I said, "Yo," using his vernacular, and we bumped fists. I provided my theory that because James Atkins supplied the food vendors, he might be here at the game, too.

"Let's check it out. Follow my lead." He ditched the cigarette at a garbage can. We worked our way through food trucks until Lance came to a compact, windowless motorhome with a door marked *venders only*. He drummed a fist on the door.

The door banged open and a man in a security uniform said, "What do you want?"

"We're with the vendors," Lance said with a straight face.

"Do you have a badge?"

"No, but I gotta cook up some brats and shit. And this girl, she's making lemonade outta real lemons and lots of sugar. You love those, right?"

I gave the man a smile and tried to look like I couldn't wait to work in a hot, confined food truck squeezing lemons and making change.

"No badge, no way." The man slammed the door shut.

"Well, thanks for trying, Lance," I said, although I didn't know why he wanted to get inside one of the trucks. "Maybe we should just walk around and look for James and Iceman."

He shepherded me through two blocks of vans selling everything from high-end Asian fusion and Mexican street tamales to the low-end standards of brats and hotdogs. The biting smell of hot chilis and franks roasting over charcoal grills made my mouth water.

I didn't see anyone I knew. No James. No Iceman.

We got to the stadium's security line, went through, and ascended the escalators. We stopped for two of those humongous lemonades, then found our box seats in the infield section. I also had a popcorn and Lance had a brat smothered in sauerkraut that he'd paid for from a wad of cash. We stood and sang the National Anthem—Lance placed his ball cap over his heart—and the game began. Baseball is one sport even I could follow. The game was a no-hitter until one of the players knocked the ball over the wall. The Denver stadium is known for home runs because our high altitude offers little air resistance.

I asked the gangster, "How did you get your nickname, Demented?"

"My girlfriend called me that and the name stuck." Another unlit cigarette he'd jammed behind one ear had slid down and caught on his thunderbolt earring.

"Why'd she call you that?"

"She said I sucked the soul right outta her, and I called her a skunk bitch."

"That doesn't sound nice, Lance."

He held up a hand. "I know, I know, I shouldn't 'a

said that. Her hormones were raging, I guess."

I lifted one eyebrow and put a little sarcasm in my voice. "Oh, really?"

"Yeah, she was pregnant."

I rocked back in my seat. "Lance, do you have a baby?"

"A boy. Lance, Jr." His chest puffed out.

"Why are you here with me? Why didn't you bring your family to the game?"

"We're here lookin' for Iceman, remember?"

I cringed all the way down to the toes of my new metallic fisherman sandals. I probably shouldn't be here, either. "And James," I added.

He went on, "And I gotta protect you, a member of the gang an' all."

"Honorary member," I reminded him. "Do you have a job? I mean, I regular job?" The heat rose to my face. Had I insulted him?

"I drive an Uber." He drove a dented, black Jeep with a cloth top. "But I don't skate any other members around, only TKs. You ever need to bend a corner, you call me."

"Sure, Lance." I nodded, glancing at the scoreboard. The broadcast camera swung over the cheering crowd and focused on a nice-looking man wearing a baseball jersey and ball cap and carrying a giant *number one* finger sign. He smiled, showing missing teeth, then the lens veered away to the other side of the stadium.

I clutched Lance's arm. "That was Iceman."

Chapter 15

"I saw him." Lance threw his thumb over his shoulder, indicating the next section and three rows up. The man himself was surrounded by others wearing team shirts. Who knew gang members were such big baseball fans.

I couldn't keep my eyes off Iceman during the next inning and paid no attention to the count. When the ballplayers ran off the field, Iceman checked his phone, rose from his chair, and started weaving past the other spectators in his row.

I grabbed my drink and shot off my seat to catch up to him, Lance came after me, and we all hiked up the steps to the nearest exit with Iceman in a substantial lead. Once through the doorway, Iceman disappeared among sports fans swarming around the food stalls and souvenir shops. The noise level was high from the loud speakers and the sea of people milling about. The smells of caramel corn, fudge, and cotton candy assaulted my nose. The crowd thinned and we caught a glimpse of Iceman stepping on the escalator.

We followed him down the moving staircase and out the gate. The gangster strutted up to a group of teens on the street corner who were throwing nervous glances all around. There must've been another home run because an uproar of cheers and foot stomping erupted from inside the stadium.

Lance told me, "Wait here, Del."

I hung out at the street lamp with my lemonade while Lance joined Iceman and the teens. Since we were now a distance from the noise of the crowd, my ears seemed sharper than usual, and I could hear Iceman's words.

"You want anything?" he asked the teens.

Was it my imagination, or did Iceman do a hand-to-hand exchange with the tallest of the boys? A drug deal?

This wasn't right. These boys were young, maybe just out of high school. It could be Axle over there, being led down the road of destruction.

Before I could talk myself out of it, I stomped over and elbowed my way past Lance. "What's going on here?"

All eyes shifted toward me, but Iceman's savage glare made me squirm and goosebumps rise on my forearms. Lance scowled at me, too, and I wondered for the first time whose side he was on.

Lance said, "It's cool, Del. Wait for me over there," gesturing behind us. When I didn't move, he took my shoulders and gave me a push, and I stumbled a few steps, but turned and flashed him a harsh look because I wasn't having it. Not having it at all. I emptied my lemonade cup in one gulp and stuffed it into a recycle bin.

A few feet away, James came down a couple of rickety stairs attached to a food truck selling fish tacos. He turned and locked the door, then flicked his gaze around the trucks. He stopped to stare at Iceman with a condemning glare, then continued looking around until his eyes landed on me.

My attention was pulled back to Iceman, who said,

"Nice doing business." He trotted off in the other direction away from the young men. Lance took off after Iceman. I looked behind me for James, but could no longer see him, so I followed the two gangbangers at a quick pace. I wasn't about to be left behind. Before we were half a block away, we had to slow down because cops patrolled the wide sidewalk. The three of us got out of their way by crossing the street to the parking lot, stopping short of my Fiat.

Lance said, "I wish ya wouldn't have followed us, Del, but I gotta take care of this." He turned back to Iceman. "You can't disrespect my girl, here." I think he meant me. "You and me, we gotta get down."

The two men circled each other. Neither could've had a weapon on them or they wouldn't have passed through gate security, but I'm sure they could still inflict damage. They seemed to be at a standoff, going round each other, while my shoes remained glued to the cement. This confrontation was all my fault.

All at once, Iceman spun toward me with dukes out, and that last gulp of lemonade threatened to fly up my throat.

I dove under my car, my knees and elbows stabbing into the gravel as I attempted to scramble out of the way. Someone grabbed my feet and yanked, and I hung on to the undercarriage until my fingers gave way.

I slid out swinging a tire iron, missing Iceman's knees like a *whiffed* strike out.

Lance ripped Iceman off me. I raised myself on my elbows as they took defensive stances, hunched like turkey vultures over a kill.

"You dead. Just like Haxxed. Both a' you." Iceman's eyes flamed with anger. He pointed his murderous gaze toward Lance and a silent communication took place. Then Iceman vanished between two parked cars.

Lance helped me to a stand, the heavy tire iron still in my hand. "You okay?"

"Yeah." I threw the tire iron into the backseat. I'd return it to its place with the jack under the car later.

"I'm going after him. I'll smack him good."

I stopped him with a hand on his arm. "No, Lance. Don't go."

"I can pop him a cap. Slash him up."

"No! No smacking. No slashing." I dusted off my jeans and rubbed my elbows. "I'm sorry, Lance, this is all my fault. I shouldn't've come here with you." Three uniforms sprinted across the street in our direction and my mouth went high desert on me. "Here come the cops!"

We jumped in my car and Lance hollered, "Go, go, go."

I crushed my foot to the gas pedal and Lance's head jerked back. I swung out on Twentieth Street toward the interstate, wondering if I was driving the getaway car from a drug deal.

"Did you sell drugs to those boys?" I asked once we cleared the intersection and left the officers behind.

"Del, I wouldn't do that. I'd save that for your initiation."

"*Whaa?* No." I bowled along toward the highway, trying to concentrate on traffic, my heart beating hard in my throat.

"Just kidding." Lance's laugh was deep and strong in a pleasant way.

"You got me there."

I signaled right and we entered the on-ramp to I-25. Once we merged with heavy traffic, I felt calmer among the horde of other vehicles and my heart beats slowed to a normal rate. "Iceman mentioned Haxxed? He said, *you dead, just like Haxxed*. What was that?"

"You prob'ly know what he's yakkin' about."

I flicked a glance at Lance, then centered my eyes back on the road. "The sheriff told me the victim's name was Jack Wojcik."

"Haxxed's name is Jack Wojcik. So, I'm thinking Iceman killed Haxxed. I haven't seen Haxxed since the party, but I didn't guess he was taken out. I didn't get a look at the body, remember? I didn't figure it was Haxxed, but I shoulda known Iceman done this." Anger compounded Lance's voice. He shoved his sleeves up and a vein pulsed on his forehead under his tattoo.

"I remember Haxxed, Lance. I know you were friends." I'd recognized his gang name. I knew who he was now. No wonder the body had looked familiar to me.

I'd met Haxxed several times before, including once at Kristen's coffee shop during a video game tournament. Haxxed is slang for "badass gamer." He was a gang-banger and computer hacker and drove a chocolate gray Kia Sportage, LX, an all-wheel drive. We weren't friendly and had hardly spoken, but knowing he was the dead guy with his hand and foot chopped off made tears prick my eyes.

"It's okay, Del." Lance gave me an awkward shoulder pat. "No worry. Iceman's going to pay. I'm calling him out."

"What are you saying?"

"I'm going to take him down and make him pay for what he did to my brother Haxxed. And for putting his hands on you. Haxxed is your brother, too. Iceman took out one a' ours. Del, this means war."

"Lance, listen to me. If Iceman killed Haxxed, then that proves he also kidnapped Rick, don't you think? How else would the severed hand and foot end up with Courtney? The kidnapper tried to intimidate her into paying the ransom by delivering those body parts. But she did pay, yet Iceman claims he doesn't have the ransom money, which makes no sense."

He extracted another cigarette from an inside pocket and twiddled it between his finger and thumb. "You're right. It don't add up."

The flashing lights of a police car illuminated the rearview mirror. I checked my speed, and we were traveling well under the limit, unable to move any faster in rush hour traffic. Still, I slowed like everyone else. Cars moved left and right out of my lane, and I was about to do the same, when the cruiser pulled up to my back bumper and gave a brief blast of the siren.

I zagged to the shoulder and came to a stop.

Did this have something to do with the rumble outside the ballpark? Instant panic!

Parker Smith in his dull gray suit climbed out of the police car and picked his way along the shoulder to my driver's door.

"Do you want my license and registration?"

He leaned over and said through my open window, "I need you to get out of the car, Ms. Morran. You, too, Mr. Palmero."

"Okay." I swung out as he stood to the side, and Lance unfolded himself from the passenger seat.

"I am going to have a look inside your vehicle. Is there anything I should know about?" Parker's voice was stern.

"No."

"Are there any drugs in your vehicle or on your person, Ms. Morran?"

I gave Lance a scared look. "No."

Parker saw my look and his eyes sharpened on Lance. "Mr. Palmero?"

"No, sir, that's truth." Lance didn't look nervous. He actually appeared bored as he lounged against the back bumper and played with his now ragged, unlit cigarette.

I peered through the rear window to observe Parker poke his fingers between the seat cushions. He lifted the floor mats and squeezed his shoulders onto the floor to search under the seats.

"Lance, are there drugs in my Fiat?" I hissed.

He shrugged. "Where's the love, Del?"

"Bite me." I jabbed my finger in his chest, hard, a few times.

Again with the shrug.

Parker beckoned me to the front of the car. "You're free to go. But I'm giving you this warning, you're associating with the wrong kind of person."

"Thank you, Mr. Smith, I'll remember that."

Vehicles parted as Parker inched his vehicle out into the traffic lane. He waved for me to pull out in front of him. Once we were both in traffic, he switched off his flashers. Semis belched black fumes as they resumed speed and changed lanes to power past us.

I got off at the next exit and brought the Fiat to a halt on the side of the road. I was not able to get my head around what'd just happened. Parker's words had hit me with the force of a well-aimed boot to the gut. Nothing was going how I'd expected. But what had I expected, hanging out with a gang member? I'd risked being caught up in illegal drug activity once again.

"I can't believe it. Look what you got me into. I've never been suspected of drugs before. This is unbelievable," I shouted at Lance, worried that Parker would tell Ephraim.

"That narc wasn't going to find anything. I'm not riding dirty." He raised his right hand as if swearing on it. "Iceman's the one pushing weight, not me."

"Oh, *puhleeze*." Fat chance I'd believe him. I mean, come on.

Lance said with a slight note of reproach, "I got my own ride home, Del. I called myself an Uber." He waved the cellphone in his hands.

"Fine."

He climbed out and slammed the door, making my little Fiat rock. I reentered the highway and was still grumbling a mile down I-25. Another mile more and I felt a pinch of guilt, so I took a moment to calm myself, got off at the next exit, cleared the overpass, and looped back around. I searched for Lance where I'd left him standing, but he was gone. And maybe I was a little relieved.

I should take Ephraim's and Parker's advice and stay away from the Thunder Knuckles gang. Not only was Lance a drug dealer and gangster, but he might actually be a suspect like Ephraim said. I also reminded myself that Lance was known as Demented for a reason. The guy carried around a wad of cash. He was at James Atkins' party where Rick Rearden was last seen and where Iceman may have been hanging out. He could be pretending to help me in order to thwart me. I didn't want to believe it, but I was mad and let myself entertain the idea.

Lance was annoyed with me, and Iceman was out to get me. Iceman was a scary dude. Both were. And now I'm without gangland protection, if I ever had it. I fought the urge to give in to fear.

Halfway up Floyd Hill, having escaped thick traffic and now able to zing along at the speed limit, I received a call from Code Enforcement to remove a car from the side of the road in Spruce Ridge. I answered on Bluetooth and told the officer, "I can tow the stall if you can wait half an hour. That's the soonest I can get there."

"No problem. The other guy couldn't haul it until tomorrow."

"Oh." I hated not being the first choice, but was glad for the job anyway. I needed to chill, and getting back to work would do that.

I picked up my tow truck and had the orange-tagged Kia Sorento, all-wheel drive, hooked up within forty-five minutes. Once I'd hauled the Kia to the impound lot, I released the towing mechanism, the Kia's rear tires hit the ground with a soft *pumpf*, the claw-like things retracted, and the crossbar laid back onto the truck bed with a final squeak. I propelled the tow dollies over to the truck's undermounts and locked them in place. The familiar routine gave me my confidence back.

This is where I belonged. This is my destiny. My purpose. It may not seem much to anybody else, but this was a big deal to me. Removing hazards off the side of the road was actually performing a public service. I was doing something worthwhile, so I started to feel better about myself.

And, I'd get paid for the haul at the end of the month, and that made me feel good, too.

The sun had begun to set. There's nothing like twilight in June, when the sun started its descent behind the mountain peaks, a pink and orange palate colored the horizon, and a breathtaking blue tinted the sky. The golden slanting rays filled my heart with hope that I'd be able to figure everything out on my own. I wasn't giving up on investigating. No way. Having made the decision, finally, to distance myself from Lance made me more determined than ever.

So, when Courtney called for another ride, I answered, "Sure. But I'm in my truck."

"Perfect. Park down the street."

I motored over to Rory's and texted Courtney that I was waiting two houses away. When she didn't show up after five minutes, I got out of the truck and made my way to the Rearden's house. She remained a no-show, so I crossed the street and ambled up James Atkins' driveway.

A curtain twitched at the RV's window, showing a slice of light, then Savanah threaded her way out the door, closing it carefully behind her. The sun had dropped behind the western mountains and the sky was now black, but the lantern that hung from the awning provided illumination. The night was warm with the temperature in the high seventies.

Savanah looked like a wraith, her long peasant dress billowing around her legs and backlit by the lantern's light. "Hi, Delaney. What are you doing here?"

"Waiting for a customer and thought I'd check on you."

"Why?"

I told her, "I have a few questions about James." He'd been at the ballgame, but there was nothing remarkable about that. Perhaps I could eliminate him from my list of suspects.

"Like what?"

"Like, anything suspicious going on at the house?"

"No. I'm probably taking off in the next couple days." She stared down at her bare feet. "Now you can answer some questions for me. Tell me about Tanner. I am totally butt crazy in love with him."

I slapped a hand over my mouth. "What?"

"That's a line from a movie. Don't you watch movies? He's really, really ridiculously good-looking, like a film star."

I ignored that. "You know Courtney pretty well, I expect, being in the same movie business? Tell me about her."

"*Exsqueeze* me? I hardly know her." She met my gaze and snorted a laugh. "I will say this much, she's a piece of work."

"Why's that?"

"Have you seen her posts? She doesn't care about her husband. She's only concerned about money."

"I have seen her comments."

"Well, so has the rest of Hollywood, but her fans love her. She won't have anything to do with the likes of me. I asked her for help to break in to the movies. She just laughed. She's evil." Savanah looked over my shoulder and her eyes fluttered. "Here she comes now, the *bi-atch*. I'll let you deal with her." The hippy girl cracked open the door and squeezed back inside the RV.

Courtney emerged out of the dark. "There you are." A few worry lines cut into her botoxed forehead.

"My truck's parked down the block." I started in that direction and Courtney fell into step beside me. "You still haven't heard from the kidnappers?"

"Not a call. But something's happened. Something really bad."

Chapter 16

Courtney squinted through the trees alongside James Atkins' driveway. I was amazed she could see anything from under her lash extensions, especially since it was dark now.

"Well, what happened? Something bad? What?" I was getting impatient with this woman.

She quit scanning the trees long enough to glare at me. "Rory's missing. I think he's been kidnapped, too. Come on."

"Rory's missing?" I skidded to a stop so fast, she bowled past me. "Rory's kidnapped?"

"Nobody's seen him since Sunday. He left his cellphone and wallet on the front entryway table. His car's in the garage, but he's nowhere to be found." She continued down the curved driveway.

I ran to catch up. If Rory hadn't been seen since Sunday, does that mean he'd been missing for three days? That's an uncomfortably long time, and I felt bad I hadn't kept in touch with him. "No word from the kidnapper?" I asked.

"No."

We'd reached my truck before the news really hit me and prickles of alarm ran over my spine. We both stood frozen with our hands on the door handles. I asked over the hood, "You're sure Rory's not around somewhere? He's not in the house? It's a big house, you know. Or he could be with friends."

Courtney hissed through clenched teeth, "His phone and wallet were left behind. His dad, Randy, says he hasn't been at work. It's not like Rory to miss work. He's very responsible. He's been kidnapped, too, I tell you."

My heart lurched like a car in first gear climbing a steep road full of boulders. We both threw open the doors and hitched ourselves into the truck. I took a moment to breathe and steady my voice, then plugged the key in the ignition with a shaky hand. "Why would the kidnapper take Rory? They already got their money. Do they want more money? What's the deal?" I gave Courtney a sideways look.

"Maybe they want more." She reached behind herself to lock the door.

"The kidnapper hasn't contacted you?" I asked again.

"No."

"Call the police, Courtney."

She cast a terrified look at me. "I'm afraid to, Delaney."

"What does Rory's dad say? He's got to be concerned."

"At the moment he thinks Rory's taking some time off. I told Randy his son has a girlfriend now and he's spending time with her."

"He believed you?"

"I'm an actress."

I cranked the engine and dropped it into gear. "Where do you want to go?"

She said, "I have to get away from here, but I don't want to be followed. The paparazzi might find me."

Easing the truck out onto the street, I gazed around,

but didn't spot the lone photographer, Wyatt Tagert. "I've watched some of your movies."

"Yeah?" She gave me a sad smile.

"Courtney, in your movie *Dead or Not Revisited* there were tons of characters with chopped-off hands."

She closed her eyes and leaned her head back on the seat. "I know, I've wondered about that, too. Maybe if I hadn't been in that movie, the kidnapper wouldn't have chopped off that man's hand or foot. I can't be responsible for his death, can I? I don't even know him. I don't know why the kidnapper used him like that."

"You're not to blame. Think of all the slasher films out there. When similar crimes happen, that doesn't make the actors at fault."

"No, I suppose not." She turned in my direction and studied me. "Rory said you had a gift for solving murders. You know, intuition and deductive ability and all that. Why haven't you figured out who's taken my husband and now my nephew?"

I swallowed hard. "I guess Rory was wrong." I didn't want be reminded of how bad I was at uncovering the truth this time.

She slid down in her seat to get a good look in the side mirror. "I don't see a Subaru Outback anywhere, do you?"

"Are you worried about that photographer?"

"Wyatt's been hiding on the main road, watching for one of our cars to come out of the subdivision. He would never guess I'd turn to you for a ride. He won't suspect I'm in this tow truck, believe me."

"I believe you." A sigh escaped my mouth. I accelerated onto the main road and turned in the opposite direction from the pullout where, sure enough, Tagert's

Outback was partially hidden. I stared in the rearview mirror until I lost sight of the Outback. "He was there, but at least he's not following us."

"Told you."

I mulled over my thoughts for a long moment, then said, "Maybe we can crack this case if we work together, talk over everything."

"What do you mean?"

"You want me to solve this crime, so let's brainstorm. I could use a little help here." *A little*? Ha! More like *a lot* of help. I said, "Let's start at the beginning. Your husband was kidnapped from a party at your neighbor's house, James Atkins."

"He must've been. I'm sure Rick never made it home."

"Okay. The kidnapper called you for a ransom. Five hundred thou. The kidnapper sent you a chopped-off hand as a warning to pay up. You didn't want the hand in your possession, so you put it inside the bag of money to get rid of it, and parked behind the coffee shop as instructed, but I towed your car before the ransom could be picked up by the kidnapper."

Courtney made a sound with her tongue against her teeth, "*Tskk*."

"Then, when the first drop-off failed, the kidnapper delivered another severed body part, the foot. We made a second attempt to exchange the money for Rick. The kidnapper, wearing a clown mask, took the money, but didn't release Rick."

"All right, all right. We know all that. Did your gangster friend have any more ideas about the hand and foot? He had a theory, right? Something about an iced man?"

"Iceman, a drug dealer. Lance thinks Iceman's trying to take over the drug trafficking in Spruce Ridge. He says Iceman's trademark move is to chop off hands."

She turned to face me. "So, Iceman is the kidnapper? You did figure it out."

I shook my head. "Iceman showed up at my place looking for the money. So, he didn't receive the ransom; he wasn't the one in the clown mask."

Her face fell in disappointment. "I didn't get a look at the kidnapper because of that mask, and the get-away car didn't have license plates. Who could it be?"

"The kidnapper is sophisticated enough to use a voice distortion device over the phone."

"Anyone can get one of those over the internet."

I said, "It must be someone you know, wearing a mask, disguising his voice. And still no more calls? Why hasn't the kidnapper released Rick?"

"And why did they take my nephew?" She shoved a knuckle to her mouth and gasped back a sob.

I blinked back threatening tears myself and cleared my throat. "Let's start with Rick. It's all connected, so that's the place to begin. Rick was last seen at James Atkins' party."

"Yes," Courtney agreed. "He had to have been abducted from there."

"Drug dealers were there. What if the man who was killed and had his hand and foot chopped off was there? Jack Wojcik, also known as Haxxed. You and I talked about him earlier today at my mom's condo, remember?" Mom's party felt like a long time ago.

"Jeez. His name sounds like Axed. Like what happened to him."

I wrinkled up my nose at the bad pun. "Maybe that's

how he's connected. What if Haxxed was the kidnapper? Not Iceman, but Haxxed?"

Courtney looked thoughtful. "Was he still alive on Saturday for the ransom drop-off?"

The clues filtered through my mind. "Well, the severed hand and foot belonged to him, so no. Haxxed wasn't the one in the clown mask. I'm sure he was already dead."

"It doesn't matter because Rick would never have left the party with that guy Haxxed or the other one, Iceman. Either of them. Had to be someone else."

"They're involved, Courtney." It was obviously all tied in together.

"You think Rick was looking to score drugs." She set her jaw in a hard line.

"It's a possibility." I realized we'd reached downtown, so I took Main to First, then cut across to Front Street.

"If Haxxed was the kidnapper, then someone killed him after he kidnapped Rick."

"That would be Iceman. They argued over the money or something." I drove a couple of blocks down Front and left-turned into Columbine without knowing where we were going. My mind was busy trying to work this out. Only a part of my brain was focused on the drive. The other part was thinking about the *how*, the *where,* the *when*, the *why*…

Maybe Rick not only took drugs, but he was a cheating husband, too. Could he have been enticed into a car by the promise of a date? A hot chick beckoned and, high on drugs, he went with her? Haxxed could have been working with a woman. But, *who*? I didn't know any of the girls in the gang. Or whether any would be capable of killing Haxxed and doing everything that went along with his death. And how they would have abducted Rory, too.

With this theory on my mind, I had to ask, "Was Rick having an affair?"

"No. He wasn't. Not just no, but hell no."

"All right. But, you know what? You're next in line as the number one suspect. The spouse is always suspected in a crime like this." Why not discuss her role? She'd acted suspiciously from the start.

She huffed out a breath, outraged. "You're crazy. How can you suggest such a thing? I kidnapped my husband and killed that gangster? Why would I?"

I weighed my next words. "You could've faked the kidnapping and gotten rid of your husband in order to keep the ransom money for yourself. It's been done before. I've seen those true crime shows."

"And I suppose I did something to Rory, too? You think I would hurt my nephew?" Her back went ramrod straight and her face turned red with outrage. "You know I didn't."

I backpedaled. "I suppose not."

"Next suspect?" Her words were clipped.

"Next suspect, Parker Smith."

Her eyes lowered to slits. "Parker Smith? The drug agent? How'd you put that together?"

"He was undercover at James' party. Did you see him there? You obviously know who he is."

She flapped a palm. "I didn't notice him, but he's a narc, so what's the surprise? He was checking out drug activity."

I trotted out my theory. "He's in a perfect position to frame somebody for the kidnapping, and he could've made Haxxed's death look like a gang slaying."

She was quiet a moment, then asked, "Why would he do that?"

"I don't know…to start a gang war, pit the drug lords against each other, who knows? He's been sneaking around your house, too. I saw him there the other night. What was that about? How do you know him anyway?"

"He questioned me, that's how. And, okay, I'll concede he's a suspect. Since we've got that settled, do you want to hear my idea?"

"Yes, I do. Go ahead."

"What about James Atkins?"

"Why him?" I buzzed down my window for some fresh air. The night was still and comfortable, and low clouds on the horizon reflected the moon.

"His party. Proximity."

"What's his motive? Why take both Rick and Rory?"

She sagged a little. "I don't know, but all your theories have holes, so don't criticize mine." There was a note of frustration in her voice and I could understand that.

"I agree. And none of our ideas account for the severed hand and foot." I continued with my train of thought, "So, let's go back to the gangsters. What if Iceman and Haxxed were in on the kidnapping together? They argued. Maybe Haxxed got greedy. They didn't trust each other because they're not in the same gang. They're rivals. Whatever. Iceman decided to eliminate Haxxed, then he used the body parts to intimidate you. So, Haxxed is dead and gone. Iceman failed to collect the money. Someone else did."

Courtney waved one hand around in small circles. "But, that doesn't fly. Rival gang members don't work together. I learned all about gangs when I did that movie, *Gangs Dead or Die*."

I thought about that. "Okay, fair enough." I stared out the windshield at the passing scenery for a moment. "So, how about this? Haxxed is the kidnapper all on his own, and Iceman heard about it and killed him to take over the kidnapping operation as part of his bid to control the territory. He started whacking off Haxxed's hands and feet to scare you into giving *him* the money, not realizing you didn't know he wasn't the real kidnapper." I liked this theory. It made the most sense.

"I hate to think a person like that has Rick tied up somewhere." Courtney gave a whole body shiver. "What about your gangster friend? Could he be the kidnapper?"

"Lance? He has an alibi for the drop-off. He was with us when you gave the clown the money, remember?" I'd actually considered him myself and whether he could've had an accomplice pick up the cash. There was always the possibility any of the suspects had an accomplice, and therefore alibis didn't matter, which made this whole exercise futile. My brain was stalled, but I didn't want to admit it. "Well, I guess we need to give this more thought. Where do you want to go now?"

"Home." She sighed.

I turned the truck toward the mansion. The night was pitch black; the only light was from houses dotting the mountainside. Headlights lit up the road in front of us, then the circles of light drew past and disappeared. When I entered the exclusive subdivision, Tagert's Outback had vanished, too.

****

The next morning, Axle suggested we stop for a coffee at Roasters on the Ridge before heading out, and it didn't take much convincing for me to agree. We'd already fed Boss, taken him for a quick walk, and left him snoring on the couch. Entering the coffee shop immediately plunged us into the comforting scent of coffee—acrid, nutty, strong—wrapping us up in warmth. Axle opted for his usual caramel latte, and I picked up an espresso. Since we had a few minutes to spare, he and I settled onto chairs at a table near the window and he toyed with his phone.

Kristen brought her own drink over and gave me a side hug before taking her seat. "So, you survived your mom's party yesterday."

"Tell me about it. You taking a break?" I slurped down a piping-hot swallow and made room for her at the table. No one was waiting in line at the counter since the place was in between rushes and nearly deserted.

"I have a minute."

I slouched down, my butt on the chair's edge. "I didn't see any bug infestations at my mom's place."

"No, the condo was really nice and clean, and it looked like everyone was enjoying themselves."

Axle plugged in his earbuds and I could hear a tinny sound coming from his direction. A number of teens pushed through the door, all wearing black tees and jeans and carrying heavy-looking backpacks, probably stopping for coffees before school. Kris rose from her seat, but I stopped her to ask, "You want a hand?"

"Thanks, but I got this, Delaney." She hustled back behind the counter.

"I heard that."

I turned to Axle. "Heard what?"

"Asking if she needed a hand." His earbuds were out.

I drew my eyebrows together. "Trying to follow that."

"A hand? A hand?" Axle made a chopping motion near his wrist.

"You goofball." I gave him a flick to the ear.

He ducked away, a smile twitching at the corner of his mouth. "You know this is getting out of hand."

I ignored him. Mostly because I didn't have a comment ready.

The loud teens congregated at the pickup counter, laughing with voices raised while waiting for their drinks. I scraped my chair closer to Axle's. I explained that Haxxed was the name of the dead man behind the dumpster, then asked, "Have you seen anyone suspicious hanging around our apartment?"

Axle was about to take a drink, but paused with his coffee cup dangling in midair. "No. Why?

"Because Iceman showed up here and threatened me, remember?"

"I remember. Did you ever tell Lopez about that?"

"No, but I told Lance."

"Slick." He nodded.

My espresso cooled on the table, so I took another sip, then added in an undertone, "I was with Lance when we tracked down Iceman at the baseball game yesterday—"

"The win, 3 to 2?"

"—Yeah, I guess. Iceman sort of threatened me again."

"What'd he say?" In spite of his thinking this some kind of a thrill, a small sliver of fear passed over Ax's face.

The noisy teens busted out the door, and the room got quiet. Sierra, one of the baristas, came out front to spritz the tables with vinegar water. Kristen must've retreated to her office in the back because she was no longer in sight. I leaned closer to Axle so he could hear my whisper.

"I'm dead. Like Haxxed."

Chapter 17

The coffee shop, usually my safe place, felt unprotected with its large plate glass windows and wide open door. Iceman's threats were all too real and he could show up here at any moment.

Axle said, "Okay, no fooling around, you need to lay it on the line for Lopez. The cops should take over. You're not doing a *Die Hard*."

"*Jeez*, okay, okay." This wasn't the first time I'd heard the lecture to quit investigating. I just didn't expect it from this immature teen.

"Swear? You'll tell Lopez about Iceman?"

"Promise." I made a cross-my-heart motion. "Now you need to promise me something."

"What?"

"That you'll be careful, too. Iceman knows where we live."

"Good point." He didn't blow me off like he usually did. The fact that Axle was worried made me worried, too. I didn't want anything to happen to my lil' cuz'.

When I dropped Ax at Oberly Motors, he reminded me, "You're going to call Lopez. Do it now."

"I will." I urged him with a go-on look. He set off at a brisk pace toward the auto bay.

So, as hard as this was to admit, the little twerp was right. It was dangerous to keep this information to myself. I'd brainstormed, I'd questioned witnesses, I'd put myself at risk. Maybe Axle too. No more. There's a murderer out there somewhere. And a kidnapper. And they could be one and the same. I should've told all this to the sheriff by now, and whether or not I was mad at him, our personal issues had no place here.

Besides, he might just share information.

When Ephraim picked up my call I asked him, "Can we talk?"

"Of course. What's the matter?" His concerned voice defeated any reserves I had left. He obviously cared about me. Ephraim was a nice guy and pretty darn good catch, that is if you like the good-looking, protective sort of guy, and who doesn't?

Where to begin?

I blurted out, "There's a new drug lord in town. Iceman."

"I know that, Delaney. We know about Iceman. Parker Smith's been looking for him. We know about Mr. Rearden's kidnapping and a possible drug connection."

My jaw went slack. "How do you know about that?"

"What with bags of money in the car and the husband *AWOL*. We could never get a hold of Mr. Rearden."

"Did Courtney tell you about the severed hand and the foot?"

"Mrs. Rearden will not talk to us about her husband's disappearance. We've questioned her several times and she refuses to comment. This happens in cases where the kidnapper intimidates the family to keep silent. Parker Smith has also met with her several times, but she won't open up to him, either. We knew she had the hand, of course, but not the foot. She found the foot, too?"

"Yes. The kidnapper delivered the hand first. Courtney put the hand in with the bags of money to get rid of it, but I interrupted the ransom exchange when I towed Rick's Volvo. They sent her the foot before the second pay-off, but Rick hasn't been released."

"When was the second pay-off?"

"Saturday, the day you returned the money to her. Courtney didn't see the kidnapper's face because the person wore a clown mask. She said he might have been five-foot-eleven or so and slim."

"He? So, male?" Scratching sounds could be heard over the phone like he was taking notes.

"Courtney said it was hard to tell. The kidnapper used a voice distortion device over the phone and didn't speak a word at the drop-off." Instead of exchanging information, I just went on to spill all I knew…the foot in the freezer, the scary Iceman, the neighbor's party, Rory missing. All of it. Ephraim hadn't known about Rory and took that bit of news seriously.

I remembered to ask, "What did you learn from the autopsy report?"

"Mr. Wojcik had been dead for several days before you found him, Delaney."

"Right. I never thought he could be the one who collected the money. But I thought he could be the kidnapper."

"Mr. Wojcik was a member of the Thunder Knuckles gang, just like Mr. Palmero. The Thunder Knuckles have never been involved in kidnapping. We're certain his death was the result of a turf war."

Why did I let myself think for a moment Haxxed could be the kidnapper? He was too tall. He was too stocky. He was too dumb.

"So, if the Thunder Knuckles aren't into kidnapping, you agree Lance Palmero wasn't involved, either?" I asked.

"There's always a possibility, but I concur."

"I'm relieved about that. The gang life is such a waste. That poor guy with his hand and foot cut off." My throat constricted. My life had intersected with Haxxed's, but I didn't help him then and he's beyond my help now.

"I can't believe you feel sorry for a gangster, Delaney. These people are law-breakers and felons."

I nodded, but still felt a dark blanket of grief on my shoulders. Death and mutilation had happened to someone I knew, if only briefly. "What can I do to help you, Ephraim? And please don't say I need to stay out of the way. Courtney talks to me. Maybe I can learn something more. Something to connect Haxxed to Rick or another clue that will identify the kidnapper."

"Well, since she's not talking to us, if she tells you anything more, I'd be grateful for a report back. But stay away from Lance Palmero. Please, Delaney. Do this for me."

I said, "Oh, sure, sure." I smiled to myself. He hadn't told me to stay away from Courtney.

"I mean it. Be serious. Especially with a second kidnapping victim."

"I am." I really meant it this time. The thought of Rory missing wiped the smile from my face.

I was still contemplating all this when it was time to leave for the tow-away zones.

This ski town was being transformed by brew pubs, and the most popular spot to park was behind the brewery, so I stationed my truck there. It was one of those crisp Colorado evenings that made you love the west, with sunrays slanting through low clouds on the horizon. I lowered my window to let in the breeze. Tendrils of my hair escaped my braid and tickled my neck.

I took a moment to bask in the silence and warmth of the truck cab. I was sitting there thinking, now what?

Ephraim had given me the go-ahead to dig deeper into Courtney's life, or rather he hadn't told me not to, so I might as well give it a try. An internet search on my phone brought up several websites, most of them of no value, until I spotted a comment that she had an uncredited appearance in an award-winning movie, *Relentless People*. The picture was about a kidnapping, and according to the movie site, Courtnee Clyborne was in a crowd scene.

The alley was empty and I had nothing better to do, so I propped my phone sideways on the steering wheel to watch the film. I paused it a couple of times to move from my spot and patrol the alley, but downtown was dead. No one was around. No alley traffic. Not even rats at the dumpsters. Nothing to be seen.

I didn't catch a glimpse of Courtney in the movie either, but the film made the time go faster, and I chuckled to myself at the funny scenes in spite of my worries about my friend, Rory.

I drummed my fingers against my lips, thinking, thinking. If only life was like in the movies, where crimes are silly capers, kidnappers are friendly people, and everything turns out right in the end. You couldn't help root for the kidnapper in the movie, *Relentless People*, who was wearing a clown mask just like in our case. Too funny.

Good. God.

Mental forehead slap.

The *Relentless* kidnapper was wearing a clown mask! A clown mask! (In case you didn't catch that clue the first time.)

Our kidnapper had obviously watched the movie. The crime was committed by someone familiar with Courtnee Clyborne's roles. And just like in the movie, the kidnapper wasn't only after money. Courtney was an influencer. Someone was trying to suck up to Courtney…maybe for a part in a picture. And, when rebuffed, pulled the kidnapping for revenge.

Could it be Savanah Rivers? The walking encyclopedia of movie lines who seemed to have seen every movie made.

I dialed Ephraim back up and when he answered, I said, "I didn't think to tell you about Savanah Rivers. She was at the party. She's living in a camper across the street from Rory where the party was held. And I think she's involved in the kidnapping. Can you get a search warrant?"

"I need probable cause. What do you have?"

"She trying for a part in a movie. She's been hanging around."

"That's all you got?"

"Yeah." I didn't think he would understand the whole clown-mask-clue. I know you got it, but would he? So the clown mask's been done before. What of it?

"I need more than that. Please keep your distance from her if you really think she's involved, and I'll look into it. Stay out of danger, Delaney."

"Okay, thanks." I disconnected, then punched in

Parker Smith's number. Maybe a drug enforcement officer would be able to get a search warrant even if the sheriff couldn't. I said when we connected, "Mr. Smith, do you remember Savanah Rivers from James' party? She's living in an RV in his driveway."

"Yes?"

"I think she may be involved...*erm*...with drugs?" My voice rose in a question. "Can you get a search warrant for her RV?"

"What proof do you have? Did you see drugs in her RV? Did you see any on her person?"

"No."

"You can't make wild accusations about people. That could be dangerous."

Not him, too.

I hung up.

Since nothing was happening here, why couldn't I check to see if Courtney was around and what she was up to? Ask a few discrete questions, like I'd discussed with Ephraim. He'd given me the go-ahead to talk to Courtney. And I'd just take a quick peek to see if Savanah's camper was still in James' driveway. She mentioned leaving for California soon. There's nothing dangerous in making sure she hadn't taken off.

I arrived in front of Rory's house within minutes. Courtney didn't answer the door at the guesthouse. My shoulders sagged in defeat, but there was still the RV to check.

Before I headed over there, I took a moment to consider what I was about to do. No, really, I did.

Neither Ephraim nor Parker seemed interested in Savanah as a suspect. They probably thought the movie-crazed hippy couldn't possibly be a criminal...and they were probably right.

But what if she'd left town? I simply had to check.

So, I hiked up the long, curved driveway. Black evergreen trunks rose into the sky and a scent of wood-burning fireplaces filled the air. Since it was getting late, clumps of stars and a half-moon slid in and out of view behind the low clouds. I came to the point where I could see the yellow-striped RV with its blacked-out louvered windows.

So, she hadn't left.

I wish I could sneak a look in one of the windows. Just a glance, then I'd leave. I crept up to the RV, stepping carefully so my heels didn't make a sound on the pavement, and circled the camper. It was so dark on the far side that I stumbled into one of the lawn chairs, knocking it over with a loud *bang*. I stood motionless, one foot lifted, one hand over my mouth holding my breath.

Savanah cracked the door. "Hello, Delaney. Is that you?"

I set my foot down. "Yes."

"What do you want?" The door was barely open an inch, just enough for her nose to stick out. She was definitely hiding something. Drugs. If I found proof, the police could issue a warrant.

"Can I come in?"

"Why? I mean, it's a mess in here. I'm not up for company."

"Savanah, I'm looking for some stuff, some stash, you know, for a good time. I think you know what I'm talking about. Wouldn't you rather discuss this inside? James might come out and ask what's going on."

For a moment she gave me a pop-eyed stare, then

she took a step back, slowly pulling the door open with her. I went up the steps and entered into a small kitchen decorated in 1970's orange and brown with a dinette booth big enough to seat four and drawn shutters at the windows. The living area opened to the truck cab, and a sun shade cut off the view out the windshield. The closed door in the back wall must lead to a bedroom and bathroom. The cabinetry was dark and the light dim.

"What do you want?" She clutched the beads around her neck. The kimono sleeves of her cotton dress fell back to reveal wrists adorned with string bracelets. "I don't have any drugs."

"No?"

"Of course not."

I was actually inside this buttoned-up RV. I couldn't give up. I couldn't leave now. The police may think she couldn't pull off the murder of a gang member and kidnapping of a prominent movie producer, but I had my doubts. Might she be capable of firing off more than movie quotes? I had to be sure.

I asked, "Have you seen Rick Rearden around?"

"No."

"He was kidnapped from James' party."

"Kidnapped?" She went wild-eyed and looked a bit green.

"And I think you know something about it."

"Why would you think that?"

"I have a theory. I'm sure you know Courtney had a small part in *Relentless People*. You probably know every line of that movie. You know the kidnapper wore a clown mask to pick up the money."

"Everyone knows that. It was a blockbuster hit."

"You copied that scene. You kidnapped Rick and

wore a clown mask to collect the ransom." My gaze took in her tall frame. She could be mistaken for a slim man if she wore bulky clothes. The clown mask would've hidden her hair and features and the voice gizmo distorted her voice.

"No. You're wrong."

"You kidnapped Rory, too. Why?"

"I didn't kidnap anyone." Her gaze shifted over my shoulder as if something caught her attention, then fear crossed her face.

A sound behind me turned me around. Iceman stood in the doorway. "I'm coming in." He jerked his head at Savanah and she flattened herself against the cupboard. I jumped out of the way and he shut the door, the three of us crowding the small space.

Savanah and I stared at Iceman. I was too stunned to speak.

"Give me the money, girlie." He brought out a gun.

Savanah's gaze darted to the bedroom door and she said through trembling lips, "The quote's not give me the money, it's show me the money. And I don't know what you mean. What money?"

"The money, the money. You know what I'm talking."

"The booty." I tried to hurry her along as goosebumps raced down my arms. "The ransom money."

"Yeah, that money," he said.

Savanah glanced at the bedroom door again. "How do you know I have the ransom money? You could be the kidnapper."

"Funny girl. I ain't no kidnapper. And I don't know what you're talking about. Who was kidnapped?"

I said to Iceman, "Rick Rearden. And I guess his nephew, Rory, too."

"I know nothing about that."

"Why are you here for the money, then?" I asked.

"I heard about the bags of money found in the backseat of that Volvo. This is my territory now and a piece of that action belongs to me." He stabbed a thumb to his chest which expanded with importance. "I don't know about any kidnapping, but I want that money."

I asked, "If you don't know about the kidnapping, do you know who killed Haxxed? Was that you?"

"I didn't kidnap no one and I didn't kill Haxxed, but I did chop off his hand and foot. I admit to that part." He said this as if it was no big deal.

"Wait, you didn't kill Haxxed? If you didn't, how'd you chop off his hand and foot?" I was trying to make sense of it.

"Okay, little girl. Let me explain it to you." He'd puffed himself up once more. "You see, James Atkins killed him. James invited Haxxed to his big, fancy party, so I showed up too. Haxxed was acting like James' muscle, all up in everyone's face. I was hanging out and saw James mixing it up with Haxxed in the back yard by the pool. They were having words about the distribution business. I thought that was interesting, so I stuck around. James stabbed Haxxed, then hid his body behind his house. He was probably planning to dump the body later, but I went and snatched it. Thought it would give me some leverage, that James would be more willing to do business with me now I've taken over." He seemed proud to tell us this.

"James Atkins killed Haxxed!" I couldn't have been more surprised at this news than if I was told to tow a car upside down. "And they were in business together?"

"Yeah. See, James sells the dirty out of his food trucks. Haxxed controlled the product. They were in business together until they had a disagreement."

"Let me get this straight. James was dealing drugs supplied by Haxxed. They argued, and James stabbed Haxxed and hid his body. You grabbed the body, chopped off his hand and foot. Then you put the body where I'd find it in the tow-away zones."

"You're truthin' it. I filed off his fingerprints, so's he couldn't be identified, and then I thought I'd better get rid of the body, too. I didn't want that slaying blamed on me. I don't want no war with the TKs."

My mouth flew open. "One person was killed and another person was kidnapped at the same party? Two separate crimes at the same place and time."

"It can happen." He smiled, showing the wide gap where teeth were missing.

"If you didn't know Courtney's husband was kidnapped, what did you hope to gain by sending her that hand and foot?" I asked him.

"Well, actually, I gave the hand to this girl here." Iceman bowed toward Savanah cowering against the built-in cabinets. "What happened was, the morning after the party I ran into Savanah outside Roasters. I was getting my morning latte—"

"—You go to Roasters?"

"Sure, everyone goes to Roasters. So, I ran into Savanah, and her and I get to talking about the party and all, and she asks me…well, you tell it, girl."

Savanah swallowed hard and shook her head, no.

He continued, "She asked me for advice."

"What kind of advice?" I gave Savanah a stern look.

She said in a small voice, "Well, you can tell this man's a power broker, so I asked him how to get someone to do what you want."

"Power broker?" I flicked my gaze back at Iceman in disbelief.

She explained, "Haven't you seen *Casino*? *Goodfellows*? Iceman told me that to get people to do what you want, you threaten them. Then he showed up at my RV and gave me the chopped-off hand. I thought it was fake. It was cold and waxy."

Iceman took up the story. "I followed Savanah over to that guest house where Courtney is staying, and I saw her leave the hand on the patio table. It was easy to see who Savanah was threatening. I figured this girl, here, was after those bags of money, same as me, and I came up with the idea of sending Courtney the chopped-off foot, too, to convince her to give *me* the money. I thought that bitch would give me the dough if I showed her strength. There was supposed to be a note delivered, too, but my bagman forgot to put the note in the box with the foot. You can't trust anyone to do the job right."

I asked, "So, why did you show up at my place looking for the money if you thought Courtney had it?"

"I heard you appropriated some of that cash for yourself—"

"—I did not."

"So I had to wonder if you had *all* the money. I knew you an' Courtney hung out together, since you've been giving her rides in your tow truck—"

"—You saw Courtney in my truck? She'll be mortified."

"Anyways, I thought since you and her seem to know each other, I'd check in with you. And that's why

I followed you here today."

"I never took any of the money."

He looked confused. "So who's the kidnapper then? It wadn't me. I was only after the bags of money. That's all I thought Savanah wanted, too."

Our eyes cut to Savanah.

"What?" She'd turned pale. "I told you I didn't do it."

"What's in the bedroom?" I pinned her with a glare. "Or should I ask, who?" We all stood still and listened real hard. Faint bumps and scrapes could be heard behind the closed door, like those muffled noises you hear from inside a sound-proof limousine.

She collapsed onto the dinette bench and stared at the ceiling. "All right. It was me. I'm the kidnapper. It's actually a relief to tell you." She gave a strained bark of a laugh.

I looked at Iceman and our eyes locked. He was evil enough to be a kidnapper and killer, but it wasn't him this time. In spite of the chill sliding down the length of my spine, I had to come up with a plan. I had to figure out a way to free Rick, and I imagine free Rory, as well, and escape from these two crazies. I could do this. I would do this. I poked my hand in my purse to feel around for my phone.

The gangster turned his gaze to Savanah. "You, hand over the cash." He swiveled to me, "You, quit looking for your phone." Then back to Savanah, "Cash, now."

Sudden banging on the outside door almost propelled me out of my skin.

"Open up! Police!"

The door flew open and Ephraim barged in with his

gun drawn and Parker on his heels. "Put down your weapon."

Iceman directed his gun at me. "No, you put your gun down, or I'll shoot her."

"Me? Why me?" I bounced both hands off my chest. Why did I always draw the attention? "You can't shoot me. I'm an honorary member of the Thunder Knuckles."

Ephraim and Parker stared at me as if I'd lost my mind. They both spoke at once. "What?" and "No way."

"Just honorary, I haven't been initiated yet."

"Oh, Delaney, I didn't know." Iceman set the gun at his feet and raised his hands. "I…I didn't know you're with the TKs. You tell Demented I didn't kill Haxxed. I only chopped off his hand and foot *after* he was dead. You'll tell him, won't you?"

OMG. A tough guy like Iceman is afraid of Demented!! More afraid of Demented than the drug squad or the sheriff. Maybe I should be afraid of Demented, too.

Ephraim kicked Iceman's gun out of the way, snatched cuffs from his duty belt, spun Iceman around, and clapped them over his wrists. "I told you to keep your distance, didn't I, Delaney?"

"Well…"

Ephraim and Parker spoke in unison, again, "Didn't I say stay out of danger?"

"Neither of you took me seriously." I folded my arms and leveled my gaze at them, but couldn't work up a decent glare. "Savanah's the kidnapper. And James Atkins killed Haxxed."

They both blinked at me, speechless.

"Why did you two show up here, anyway?" I was glad they did, but I pretended outrage. I may not have guessed about James—who could?—but I was right about Savanah. And mostly right about Iceman. I should never have doubted myself.

Ephraim said, "Parker called me after you asked him for a search warrant. I told him you'd asked me for the same thing, so we decided to do a drive-by and saw your truck. Then we observed Iceman entering the RV. Well, you got what you wanted because that gave us probable cause to come inside." He turned to the narcotics officer. "Parker, can you detain Ms. Rivers?" He jerked Iceman out the door and down the steps, speaking into his mic, "I need backup. Two suspects in custody, and one at large, James Atkins."

Parker captured Savanah's right wrist in a handcuff.

I asked her, "The men are in the bedroom, right?"

She said, "I wanted to lock them in the basement like in *Relentless People*, but I didn't have a basement, only the RV."

I thought back to the timing of the kidnapping. "When Tanner towed this RV, was Rick inside?"

"Yes."

"That's illegal. You can't tow an RV with a person inside."

Parker said, "Let's have a look." He clicked her left handcuff to the table leg and reached the bedroom door in two strides. It was locked, but one kick put a hole through the light wood. Two men were bound and gagged on the bed.

When Parker loosened the gags from their mouths, Rick and Rory smiled the same lopsided grin. Rory said, "Thank God you found us."

While Parker was ripping off the bindings around their hands and feet, I stepped back to the front of the

RV. I had to ask the kidnapper, "How in the world did you tie up two men?" She's tall, but super-model thin, not more than a hundred-twenty pounds, if that.

"Well, you know…" She had the grace to look embarrassed.

I tried not to roll my eyes. "Why didn't you let Rick go after you collected the money? And why tie up Rory, too?"

"I was still holding out for a movie role. That's all I really ever wanted, a part in Rick's next film. I asked for the money, but I told him I would take the part over the money. He said no. And after that, since Rick could identify me, I didn't know what to do. I thought if I got Rory in here and tied him up, too, that Rick would give in, but he didn't."

"If you had the money why didn't you leave town and hide out somewhere? I mean, the money is as good as a part in a movie, right?"

"I was hoping for my big break, then I'd have lots of money. But after I got the money I was worried leaving town would be suspicious, plus I was trying to get Tanner to go with me, but he wouldn't."

"Why did you hand Courtney a clown mask at the drop-off?"

"I guess because of the movie, I don't know. I don't know why I did any of it. What was it all for?" Her voice grew whiny. "In *Relentless People* the kidnappers get what they want and the kidnap victim even helps them. Rick did nothing like that for me. And now I've been caught."

Chapter 18

Within minutes several black and white patrol cars arrived with red and blue strobes flashing. Wyatt Tagert, who materialized out of nowhere, snapped some pictures.

Wyatt came over to me. "What happened?"

I signaled toward Savanah, restrained in the back of a police cruiser. "Savanah's been arrested for the kidnapping of Rick Rearden and his nephew, Rory." Then I waved a hand toward Ephraim escorting James out his front door. "James Atkins has been arrested for killing a drug dealer, Haxxed." Then I swiveled to where Iceman was locked in Parker's gray Fusion. "Another drug dealer, Iceman, has been arrested for chopping off Haxxed's hand and foot. At least I think that's why he was arrested."

Parker approached us. "Who are you?" he asked Wyatt, who was scribbling in a tiny notepad.

The photographer gave him his card. "I work for *Muckamuck Magazine*. Can you confirm the charges against these people?"

"That will be up to the DA."

"Can you tell me off the record? I never reveal my sources."

Parker nodded. "Off the record. Delaney was right about the charges against Savanah Rivers and James Atkins. As far as Iceman, we'll get him for tampering with a dead body and menacing with a deadly weapon."

"Who did he menace?" I asked.

"You. He pointed a gun at you and threatened your life."

"Oh, yeah."

An ambulance zoomed up, almost jumping the curb, and paramedics assisted Rick and Rory into the back. Parker left us to join the first responders.

Wyatt asked, "Why did Savanah kidnap the Reardens?"

"She did it for a part in a movie, not for money, can you believe that? Courtney gave her half a mil'."

"I remember the cash you found in Rick's Volvo. That was the ransom?"

"Yes, and I never helped myself to any of that money."

"So, this was all over a role in a film?"

"That's right."

He gave out a low whistle. "You can't make this up. It'll be a great story."

"Too bad she'll never get a part now. She'll never make it to Hollywood." I smiled.

Or Tanner, either. Shame, that.

****

I was too excited to get much sleep that night, so early the next morning, while yawning my head off, I hightailed it down the stairs to Roasters on the Ridge. I didn't even wait for Axle who was still in the shower. He'd know where to find me. I gulped down my latte and ordered another, although the last thing I needed was more espresso.

Wired, much?

Demented ambled through the door with a magazine

folded under one arm, spotted me, and came right over. Obviously, he was here to see me.

"Del."

"Demented."

"So, we're back to Demented, are we?" He showed me the paper. "You see this?"

I angled my head to read the title of the article, "Tow Truck Driver Rescues Movie Producer." I snagged the magazine out of his hand and turned over to the front page. It was *Muckamuck Magazine*. Then I skimmed the article written by Wyatt Tagert. He not only told the story that I solved a kidnapping, he stated the truth about the money—that I did not take any cash from the bags. He mentioned an unnamed nephew (Rory) in the last paragraph. Hopefully I wouldn't have to suffer through any more snide remarks about helping myself to some of the loot.

"You never told me Haxxed was James Atkins' drug supplier. I might've put it together sooner."

"I was gonna tell you after your initiation. You need to be truly one of us before we share that stuff." Demented reached into a pocket and came out with a little gift bag tied with a bow. "Something for you for avenging Haxxed. You done this twice now, Del."

"I can't take your gift."

"It's just a pair of earrings. Lightning bolt earrings." He fingered a lightning bolt earring dangling from his own earlobe.

I thrust the bag toward him. "Really, I can't."

"Why not?" He wore a trace of a scowl.

"What I say might make you mad."

He laughed. "No worries, Delaney. I don't chop off nobody's hands. I'm not like Iceman."

No, Demented was an even bigger bad boy, one that put fear in Iceman's heart.

"Okay, this is what I have to tell you. I don't want to be an honorary member of the Thunder Knuckles. I respect you and the brotherhood and how you take care of each other, and I understand about family ties, but you deal drugs and kill people."

"I mostly kill other criminals."

"I can't be a part of that. You're going to end up in jail or worse, dead."

"But other than that?"

"Demented, you need to get out of the gang. Drugs are bad and destroy families and communities. And I love this town. I don't want gangs to infiltrate my town. No offense."

"None taken."

I never tried to help Haxxed, and now that he's dead I'll never get a chance, but maybe I could help Demented. I pointed toward Kristen behind the counter. "You should talk to Kristen. She has all kinds of resources. She can find someone to help you." Kris's church assisted people with addiction problems. Kris volunteered at the women's shelter and the food bank and did all kinds of good works. She would know what to do.

"I'll think about it. Well, that's it then. Bye, Del." He texted somebody, then gave me a salute before leaving.

I thought that'd be the last I'd hear of the Thunder Knuckles, but it wasn't. You're not going to believe this, but…Parker Smith called to tell me the news that not only was Iceman's gang run out of the area, but Demented moved his gang out of town, too. Demented sent out orders that Delaney Morran—me!—wanted the town cleaned up, so he pulled the troops and the TKs had left Spruce Ridge.

About James Atkins. His being the murderer was such a shock, *amiright?* But he confessed to killing Haxxed in an argument about the drug business. By the way, he claimed he didn't know about the kidnapping or that Rick and Rory Rearden were locked up in the RV in his driveway. I'm not sure anyone believed him.

And that blonde I saw with Ephraim at the mall? Turned out she's Ephraim's younger brother's girlfriend. Ephraim was shopping at the mall and stopped by where she worked to say hello. Lopez was surprised I would suspect him of anything more. I was surprised Lopez was shopping. So, we're back together.

I'm happy to report Will sent Mom flowers—after I'd given him the name of a florist and nagged him ten times. She put the condo up for rent and moved back home. *Yippie I oh, yippie I aye!*

I still can't believe Savanah was the kidnapper. I mean, *I* was the one who figured it out and everything. But still. What a curveball. I was such a good friend that the next time I saw Tanner, I didn't rub it in.

And as for me, when Mike Horn needed a tow man to move a Porsche 918 Spyder, this high-heeled tow woman responded to the call. That's a mid-engine plug-in hybrid sports car that can alternate between front-wheel, rear-wheel, and all-wheel drive, and I knew all that without looking it up.

Once I had the rear wheels on the tow dollies and the front wheels on the T-bar, Mike Horn stepped out onto the concrete platform behind his coffee shop and traipsed down the cement steps toward me. "Thanks for your help, Delaney."

"You're welcome, Mike." I strapped the vehicle's wheels down, trying to look like a professional vehicle recovery agent. In reality I was trying to keep my ankles from giving out in my platform heels.

He said, "Good job ridding this town of a drug dealer, too."

"Well, let's hope another drug crew doesn't move in."

"At least you took care of the last one." He gave me a thumbs up.

Did I take care of the Thunder Knuckles or did they take care of me? Demented's gang had left town. Iceman was behind bars. A kidnapper and a murderer were, too. Spruce Ridge felt safe again.

"And thanks for removing this car."

"Yeah, people really shouldn't park in a tow-away zone. What are they thinking?" I shook my head.

Then I climbed inside my Fulcan Xtruder with the Porsche secured on the back.

Together we spun away into the night.

A word about the author…

Karen C. Whalen is the author of two cozy mystery series, the Dinner Club Murder Mysteries and the Tow Truck Murder Mysteries. The first in the dinner club series, Everything Bundt the Truth, tied for First Place in the Suspense Novel category of the 2017 IDA Contest. In the Tow Truck series, Eyes on the Road was a Second Place winner of the 2023 Firebird Book Awards in the Cozy Mystery category. Whalen loves to host dinner parties, camp, hike, and read.

Thank you for purchasing
this publication of The Wild Rose Press, Inc.

For questions or more information
contact us at
info@thewildrosepress.com.

The Wild Rose Press, Inc.
www.thewildrosepress.com